Abandoned Archives

By

Creative Writing Students of
La Quinta High School

La Quinta High School
Westminster, California

Abandoned Archives

ISBN: 978-1-7322309-3-4

Edited and Compiled by: Amanda LaPera

Senior Copy Editors: An Huynh, Bryce Le, Brian Ly

Senior Section Editor: An Huynh

Section Editors: Khanhlam Doan, Keanu Hua, Bethanie Luu, Hillary Nguyen, Kayla Nguyen, Khanh Tran

Cover Designed by: Vi Bui

Interior Editor: Khanh Tran

Published by La Quinta High School Creative Writing Class

Dedicated to those who persevere through harsh times

PREFACE

Entering into the new year, we hoped that the struggles of 2020 would have been far behind us, yet the quarantine persisted. Even with the more stable and regular meetings relative to those of our last anthology, our work piled on higher and our time dwindled before we knew it.

From the standpoint of our section editors, familiarizing with the flow of the system was difficult and slow. From the standpoint of our copy editors, responsibilities grew ever higher as they ushered everything into progression. And from the standpoint of our interior and cover designers, finishing the book lay in their hands which were tied until the very end.

But here we are, finally past the end.

Through all the hardship, stress, and obstacles, the La Quinta High School Editing Team persevered to offer you the fruits of the 2021 Creative Writing Class's efforts.

—Brian Ly, Senior Copy Editor

Table of Contents

An Obligation

by Brandon Nguyen

For every man that yells,
His voice is heard
For every woman that screams,
Her voice is heard
With voices so loud,
They cannot be turned down
They tell you to do this
And tell you to do that,
With cries so loud that
Even the wise ones fall
Crashing down like waves
When others jump in
When others ride the tide
When others simply float along
With those who say so little
Is it not your job to stand?
Is it not your job to stay on top?
Is it not the trial of any great man
To stand above the sea?

HELL AND HIGH WATER

by Bryce Le

THE SHIP ROCKED BACK and forth on the waves. The birds in the sky above screeched to one another. The glistening sun beat down on me. I stared at the fish through the sight of my harpoon gun. Wasn't sure what type of fish, exactly, but it was rather small in comparison to the others I'd seen. The thing was only ten meters long.

I smirked. *Only* ten meters. Talk to folks who lived anywhere else in the world and they'd say ten meters was too big. But for us? Small fry. Still, it was big enough that it would survive if I didn't place my shot right.

"Steady hand, laddie." Captain Helvig placed his hand on my shoulder. "Breathe. You won't be hitting anything if you're shaking like that."

I nodded. "Aye, sir. Just nervous."

"That's natural. You'll get more comfortable as you go." He pointed at the front end of the fish. "Now remember, with a mundane harpoon gun like the one you've got, you'll want to get 'em in the eye. One shot, one kill."

"Aye, Cap'n." I exhaled and pulled the trigger. The roped harpoon shot out of the gun, burying itself into… the body of the fish. Ah, hell. It began to thrash wildly as it put on a burst of speed, pulling my gun along with it.

The gun that I was still holding. It was torn from my hands, over the railing and into the water, as I slammed into the deck. The fish dove underwater, taking the gun and my last shred of dignity along with it.

"At least you hit 'em this time," the captain said. "You're improving, laddie. How do you feel 'bout that?"

I groaned, starting to push myself up off the floor. "I'd feel a lot better if 'improving' didn't mean I can still get beaten by a fish."

He pulled me back up to my feet. "You'll get there. Any injuries?"

"Not this time, sir."

"Good, good. Wouldn't want a repeat of last year," he said. "If you're feelin' up to it, find Raum and tell him about how you lost *another* gun. Ship's docking soon, I've got to make sure we're ready for landfall."

"Aye aye, Cap'n." And with that, I was off. I weaved through the crowds on the deck, muttering vague apologies as I bumped into them. Our quartermaster shouldn't have been hard to find, considering the fact that he was the tallest person onboard. Even so, I was having trouble spotting him. A pair of heavy hands clapped onto my shoulders from behind.

Boisterous laughter filled my ears. "You're lookin' like a drowned rat, Axel. What did you do this time?"

I mustered up my best glare before turning around to face the voice. "Raum, you absolute…" The giant of a man simply kept smiling through his bushy beard. I dropped the glare. "Gun's gone, by the way. Got stuck in a fish and pulled under."

"Oh? Was it 'cause you were usin' the—"

"Why yes, it was because you gave me the *worst* harpoon gun on the ship. If I had an enchanted one, that fish would have been dead."

"You can't hit the broad side of a barn, mate. Think I'd trust ya with a 'chanted gun? One missed shot and *boom*." He spread his arms wide. "Big hole in the ship, and now we're sinking and everyone's dead."

"Good point." I quite liked this ship. Last thing I wanted to do was sink it.

"Also, recoil would probably be enough to shatter your entire arm. Better to not try it yet, yeah?"

"I—" a bell rang out, "—never mind, looks like we're back at port."

"Aye. Figure we should finish up. Cap'n ain't going to want us 'dirtying up his decks' after we dock."

"Ah, he doesn't mean it." I chuckled. "You know he cares about us."

"Just 'cause he doesn't mean it don't make it any less scary when he starts yellin'." Raum sighed. "Not like it matters, I guess. Good to be back home, no matter how much yellin' we have to take."

"Can't wait to trade in endless fish dishes for more endless fish dishes."

"It's what we get for livin' in Lysvann, mate. What, you expect the city full o' fishermen to *not* have fish?" His laughter rang out again.

"Well, view makes up for it, at least." I leaned over the deck railing, and he followed suit.

"That it does, mate."

Of course, Lysvann was more than just a normal fishing town. A normal fishing town wouldn't have a population of over 10 million. A normal fishing town wouldn't be a center of tourism for people all over the world, nor would it be the size of a small country—not that I had ever been to the more populous areas of the city. I stayed in the docks districts and on the sea, and I never saw much reason to go beyond.

Raum clapped me on the back once more before walking away. "That's enough thinkin' for today. Let's get out of here. I want to enjoy my free time."

"*You* get to enjoy your free time, maybe," I said, following him off-ship. "I've gotta help the Cap'n plan our next route."

At that, he turned around. "You really call him Cap'n even at home? You don't call him Dad or Pops or something like that?" He elbowed me in the ribs, sending me stumbling. I waved my arms around to recover my balance. "Doesn't sound very… son-like? Is there a word for that?"

I glared at him. "First off, don't do that. You want me to fall off or something?" Raum just smiled. "Not even denying it, huh?" I grumbled. "Secondly, why wouldn't I call him Cap'n? He's the captain. And finally, I'm not *really* his son, so—"

"You know damn well that he still thinks of you as one. You really haven't gotten that into your thick skull yet?"

I didn't respond. He didn't continue. We just walked down the ramp in silence, moving towards the docks. They were a lot quieter than usual, I suppose because we'd come back to port quite a bit earlier than we usually did.

It was uncomfortable, really. The place felt empty without the hustle and bustle of hundreds of people milling about, without the boasting from sailors about who caught the biggest fish that day or who was a better shot with a harpoon gun. The only people around were the dockworkers and our crew members as they waited around for Captain Helvig to dismiss them.

Raum didn't seem to be affected by the mood, though. He still had his ever-present smile, his arms swinging to the beat of some unknown rhythm. When we finally reached the end of the ramp, he sighed in contentment. "Good to be back on land again."

Captain Helvig turned to him. "Don't get too used to it, you hear? We're setting out again in a day." The crew groaned. "We're just here to make some additions to the ship and restock our supplies. You all have some free time to enjoy. Just make sure you're back on time. Dismissed."

"Aye, Cap'n." Our voices rang out in chorus. The crew broke off, spreading out as they said their goodbyes and headed back to their homes.

Raum clapped his hand on my shoulder. "See you, mate. Good luck with your old man." He chuckled as he walked off.

Eventually, the captain and I were the only members of the crew left in front of the ship. For a while, we stood in silence, simply observing the port around us. In the distance, I could see dockworkers loading shrimp the size of people onto a cart, while ocean waves crashed against the harbor rhythmically.

The captain lifted his eyepatch and took in the sea breeze. His long coat fluttered in the wind. It was a little ritual of ours, to do this when we returned to port. The sea might've been our second home, but Lysvann would always be our first.

And as a bonus, we could see how good our day's haul was compared to everyone else's.

Finally, one of us spoke. "Come on, laddie." Captain Helvig set off at a brisk pace. "We've got work to do."

I followed slightly behind him. "What are we doing now, Cap'n?"

"We're picking up something from ol' Oswald. I've been wanting to get my hands on it for a while."

On second thought, I would have preferred not knowing. Having to pick something up from Oswald was bad news. If it was something the runecarver didn't want to deliver, that probably meant that it was volatile and liable to explode, possibly also setting everything around it on fire.

As we moved further away from the docks, the serene atmosphere faded away, and muted chatter filled the air. The streets were more crowded, groups of people milling about and enjoying the sea breeze.

"Ah, we've arrived." The captain stopped in front of a large garage, windows glowing softly with light and the distinctive sound of a chisel carving into metal coming from inside. Captain Helvig slammed his fist against the door, raising his voice. "Open up."

The chiseling sound stopped, only to be replaced by what could only be described as the sound of chaos: something heavy hitting the floor, a yelp of pain, and a series of crashing noises.

The door rolled upwards revealing a man covered in ash, his clothing singed and full of holes. Behind him stood an enormous… thing covered by a sheet. Said sheet also had holes burned through it.

If I hadn't already been worried about our safety before, I was now.

The man smiled. "Magnus, Axel. How's life?" He gestured for us to enter, rolling down the doors behind us.

"Same ol'," the captain replied. "And you, Oz? How was my commission?" He glanced at the sheet.

"Nearly died five times working on it." Oswald laughed. "New record, I'd say. Come on, let's take a look." He hobbled over to the big sheet thing. "Ready? One, two—" with a flourish, he threw the sheet up, "—three. She's a beauty, isn't she?"

Sitting in the middle of the workshop was a massive harpoon cannon on a swivel base. Glowing runes covered the surface, so small that I could barely make out the individual characters. There was care put into every carving, and they all *hummed* with energy.

"Hey, Oz?" I began. "How long were you working on this?"

"Haven't slept in a week." He smiled. "By the way, Magnus, I should have asked this earlier, but... what are you planning on doing with this, exactly?"

A moment passed. "Fishing," the captain said. He didn't elaborate. What was he planning to fish up with a cannon this big? "You did a good job, Oz. I'll send some men over to haul it out later. Now then, about the payment..."

Three hours of haggling later, the captain and I left Oswald's workshop and made it home. My eyes were still glazed over from the price "discussion." Lowball offers, highball counter-offers, counter-offers to said counter-offers, something about a favor... my head hurt just thinking about it. It wasn't like we were broke or anything. Why didn't the captain just take it at the price he was offered?

Maybe this was just one of those social things I wasn't great with, but it didn't matter much to me at this point. I was more focused on helping the captain plan our next route.

We stood in the basement, in front of a map covered in markings of dozens of colors. Dates were scribbled near each line. *This* was the heart of our fishing business; after all, you can't catch fish without knowing where they are.

"We've got that new cannon," he said. "We can go for bigger hauls now."

"True, but that doesn't mean much if we don't know where they are."

"Should be right around this area," he said, circling a darker region of the sea, "around Stormheart's territory."

"All due respect, Cap'n, I'd rather not get eaten by a giant sea dragon." Why did the captain even *consider* that? Every fisher grew up hearing stories about the "Scourge of the Sea," the city-sized monster that sank damn near every ship that entered its domain. Hell, the captain himself told me those stories when I was a kid.

"Calm down, laddie. I'm not suggestin' we prance up to his front door. I was thinkin' somewhere near it, though." He laid his finger on the map, atop a place marked 'Sjova Reef.' "Like here." It was south of the dragon's territory, but still relatively close.

"Never heard of it before. Why there?"

"I was with some o' the other captains last week, and Alesund talked our ears off about how he ran into some real leviathans over there." He chuckled. "Pretty sure his exact words were 'they were bigger than a dozen of my ships.'"

"You believe him?"

"Not at all. Doesn't hurt to check, though. Here's my plan." He drew a line on the map, from our port to the reef. "We make way for Sjova Reef first. If it ends up being nothing, we'll go back to the usual place and I'll smack Alesund next time we see him. If he's right, then we'll camp out in that area for a few days. Any questions?"

"Still a bit too close to Stormheart for my liking, but…" I sighed, "better than going right up to it."

"That's settled, then." The captain grinned. "We're heading out early tomorrow, laddie. Get some rest."

"Aye, Cap'n." I gave a quick salute and headed up to my room. It was simple; nothing but a bed, a table, a closet, and a window on the far wall. Wasn't much, but it was all I needed. The stars were shining brightly tonight, and the streets of the city were lit up with lanterns.

I sat on my bed and frowned. Too quiet. It was always hard to get used to land again after a long time at sea. I slid the window open slightly and let the night breeze in, carrying with it the crashing of the waves and the never ending chatter coming from the city. That was more like it.

Hopefully we wouldn't all die tomorrow.

*   *   *

Splash.

"Oi, get up, laddie." The captain roused me out of bed. And by "roused me," I mean he dumped an entire bucket of freezing water on me.

"Did you have to do that, Cap'n?" It was funny the first time, less so the hundredth time.

"It works, doesn't it? You're up and you're awake." He smiled down at me. "Now, get up and head to the ship when you're ready." With that, he walked out the door, leaving me soaked and shivering. Eventually, the freezing cold forced me to get out of the bed and dry off.

First order of business was to get some dry clothing on. Couldn't choose anything fancy, it'd be ruined after a day on the ship—not that I owned anything fancy, anyway. I pulled open the closet door and chose from one of my three identical shirts.

I stepped out into the hall, which was a lot quieter than usual. Looked like the captain left early. If I wanted to catch up with him, I'd have to eat something fast. Well, I'd just see what food we had and figure out what to do from there. I opened our ice chest and saw a *lot* of fish. Nothing else.

Not sure what I was expecting, really, but food was food. Getting back to sea was more important, anyway. I threw a fish filet on the stove to heat it up, before running down the rest of my mental checklist. Jacket? Check. Same one I always wore. Shoes? Check. Had a hole in 'em, but they'd hold. Breakfast? Check. It tasted awful—no seasoning will do that—but it kept me from starving. Time? …No check. I had five minutes to get to the docks. And with that, I headed out and sprinted.

The streets were always crowded around this time of the morning; sailors walking down to the docks to set out to sea, lost tourists wandering the area, and workers heading to their businesses to set up for the day. I weaved my way through the crowds and cut through the alleys to make it to the ship. Most other people wouldn't be able to get there in time, but I knew this part of town like the back of my hand, and I had turned "getting to the docks" into a science.

Duck through the side street, avoid the guy mumbling to himself. Clamber up the side of that clothing store that all the tourists like for some reason. Run along the rooftops until you reach Hans' Butcher Shop, slide down the drainpipe, and then a straight dash to the docks.

I made it in four minutes and thirty seconds. The rest of the crew was just starting to board, and I stopped in front of the captain to catch my breath.

He chuckled. "Made it on time, lad. So, what do you think?"

"About what?" I asked. He raised an arm and pointed towards the ship.

Oh. Right. The harpoon cannon was mounted atop the bridge of the ship, and it looked…

I paused. How did I put this? "Awful. Honestly, looks awful, Cap'n." It looked good by itself, but it just didn't fit with the rest of the ship at all.

"Yeah, I get what you're saying. Still, if it works, it works. Let's get aboard."

I followed him up the ramp and broke off to where the rest of the crew was. Or, more specifically, where Raum was. He was easy to spot, what with the fact that he stood a full head above everyone else. I settled down next to him and waited for the captain to announce our departure.

The dock bells rang. The captain stood in front of us. His eye scanned the crowd. "All right then, looks like everybody's accounted for. Weigh anchor, men, we're setting out."

The crew exploded into action as everybody scrambled to their stations. I headed below decks with Raum to help him with the inventory. Through the labyrinthine hallways and passages of the ships, we came to a stop in front of a steel door, and stepped through. The room was covered wall-to-wall in all kinds of fishing equipment: a harpoon gun rack, piles upon piles of replacement nets and ropes, fishing rods, and, oddly, a nondescript brown box.

The ship lurched beneath us. "Looks like we're off," Raum said as he took note of the amount of nets in the piles.

"What's this?" I asked him as I picked up the box. Light, but not too light. Wide, but not deep.

"That? That's something I got for you." He grinned. "Open it up, will ya?"

"For me? Cheers, mate." I opened the box to see… "Really?"

He laughed heartily. "*Baby's First Harpoon Gun.* Thought you might need it. What do you think?"

"I think I hate you. Besides," I said, inspecting the box, "I'm not *that* bad. Wha—*for ages 5 and up?* Come on."

"Give it a go, mate. There's a target in the box. Let's set it up, why don't we?" He pulled out a massive paper fish and plastered it on the wall. "Go on, have a shot. Aim for the head."

"Fine." I huffed. I raised the "gun" to my shoulders, took a deep breath, aimed, and pulled the trigger. I missed it entirely. "Alright, maybe I *am* that bad."

"I think you're gonna need to make more use of this. Don't want to be makin' a fool of yourself again."

"Mess up a few times and you never live it down." I groaned. "Alright, let me have another go." Again, the harpoon was loaded. I aimed at the fish. I fired. Once more, the shot went wide, no closer than my last one had been.

Raum sized me up. "I think I see the issue here. You're not *focused,* mate."

"What's that supposed to mean? I'm looking at the fish, aren't I?"

"You're getting distracted too easily. Your *eyes* are looking at the fish, but your *brain* is looking at something else, and your arms are shaking 'cause of it." He tossed me the harpoon again. "Focus. Pretend there's just you and the target."

Nothing but me and the target, huh? Alright then. Once more, I raised the gun to my shoulder. "Just the fish. Only the fish. Nothin' else," I mumbled. But the instant before I pulled the trigger, the ship rocked hard and my attention flickered. The shot nailed the fish target in the fin.

"Well, at least you hit it this time, eh? You'll get there some day, mate." He grinned. "Right then, that's enough of that. We've still got inventory to take."

"Aye, aye. I'll take the left wall," I said. And so, with that bit of excitement out of the way, we moved back to doing our jobs, counting the supplies in silence. Well, relative silence. There was the occasional sigh of frustration when one of us lost count, and the clattering of a broken piece of equipment being tossed into the junk pile. But all in all, it was just another day.

Raum jotted some numbers down in his clipboard. "Final count is… forty-six nets, two dozen enchanted harpoon guns, one *normal* harpoon gun—that one's yours—and… one-hundred-and-sixty-three spare harpoons. You?"

"I've got sixty-seven lengths of rope, one spare anchor, twenty-six spyglasses, and thirty-three fishing rods. Why do we even have those? I've *never* seen anyone use one."

"We keep forgetting to toss 'em out. I'll put 'em in the junk pile later."

"We're done here then, yeah? Time to grab some fresh air?" I asked. After an hour cooped up inside the swaying hull, I was craving the sea breeze.

"Eh, sure, why not. We ain't got much better to do." Raum stowed his papers away and joined me as I walked out the door.

The ocean was remarkably calm, and the weather pleasant. Some clouds drifted overhead, and there were few, if any, waves. Nothing but the endless blue, stretching so far that I could see the curve of the world over the horizon.

This was why I loved the sea. No walls to stop you, no people coming up to tell you what you could or couldn't do. Just you and your ship, and you could go in any direction you wanted.

*   *   *

The rest of the journey to the reef was uneventful, for the most part. I didn't do much aside from swab the decks and practice my aim. Not like there *was* much to do yet, not before we got to our destination.

The ship's bell rang on the third day, and I felt the ship slow down until we were swaying only from the current. We had reached our destination. The crew shuffled below decks, grabbing their harpoon guns and nets. They'd done this dozens of times before, and they knew what to do. I wasn't with them. I was with the captain, up on the bridge and next to the giant cannon that was somehow both a beautiful work of art and a massive eyesore at the same time.

"Don't see anything," I said. "I guess Alesund was lyin' like usual, eh?"

The captain frowned. "Even if he was, there should be *something* here. This is too quiet. It's not normal." The waters were calm and still, the crew holding their guns in aiming positions as we waited with bated breath for any sign of a catch. A minute passed. Then another.

A massive fin burst out of the ocean, kicking up water and parting the seas as it passed. In unison, the crew fired, a wall of steel and rope plunging into the waters and its skin. The creature twisted and squirmed, jumping out of the water to reveal its full size. It was easily the size of our ship. I'd seen *buildings* smaller than it. Our dozens of harpoons had barely done anything but scratch it, and on any of our previous voyages, we'd have never dreamed of even *trying* to take a fish of this size down.

"Got you now." The captain grinned. He lined up the gun with his target and pulled the trigger. A deafening *crack* echoed from the cannon's barrel, and a seven-meter-long spear of enchanted steel rocketed outwards, piercing directly through its head. The fish stopped struggling, dead. It crashed into the ocean, throwing up a plume of saltwater and blood.

"Reel it in and secure it to the side," the captain commanded. "I want all our counterweights shifted to starboard." The deck burst with activity, some sailors running beneath the decks to move the weights stored at the bottom of the ship, others helping their crewmates haul the creature in. The flurry of excitement only lasted a few seconds, but it felt so much longer.

"I'll be damned," I said when my adrenaline died down. "He wasn't lying. That's a real leviathan."

"Hmm." The captain acted as if this was just another day for him. "Ship's listing a bit. That damn beast is bigger than I thought it'd be." It was a tiny change, but I could feel it. The ship was leaning ever so slightly to its port side. "Don't think we'll be able to haul another one like it, not if it's even half the size of this one."

"Turning back already?"

"This one catch will net us more than our last three trips combined. Even if we play it safe and head back now, we'll be making good profit. Besides," he said as he scanned the waters around us, "looks like the skies are darkening behind us. Get a closer look if you can, laddie."

"Aye, sir." I pulled my spyglass out from my belt and gazed south, on the path we took to get here. What I saw was… "Oh, hell."

"What is it?" The captain glanced behind him.

"Storm. It's a big one." Waves were churning up the water, thrashing about.

"How big?" The captain peered into the distance, his brows furrowed.

"Look for yourself, Cap'n."

He focused the spyglass and frowned. "Never seen anything like this." He handed it back to me and turned to the harpoon gun.

"Those waves are as tall as houses." Any wind strong enough to do that would break our ship in half in an instant. "We'll never make it through."

"Check east and west. How far does it go out?"

"Too far. I can barely see the edge of it from here. It'll hit us by the time we make it that far out."

"Damn skies were clear just minutes ago," the captain said. "Where the hell did it come from?"

"Does it matter, Cap'n?" I kept my eyes fixed on the storm. "It's picking up speed."

"How fast? Think we can outrun it, laddie?"

"Not when we're weighed down like this. That thing is going *fast.*"

"We'll cut the fish down and go full speed to the north. That'll be our best chance."

I wasn't so sure.

"North is Stormheart's, cap'n. It spots us and we're dead for sure."

"I'd rather we have a chance of getting killed by a sea dragon, instead of *definitely* getting taken out by those waves. It's either the risky option or death." He raised his voice down towards the people on the deck. "Storm incoming. Cut the fish loose, full speed ahead. We're making a break for it."

The crew didn't question his orders. They never did. With practiced motions, they sliced the fish's bindings, and we began to list starboard before the crewmates belowdecks shifted the weights once more. The ship lurched forward, the engines spinning to life at maximum power to propel us away.

I returned my gaze to the storm behind us. It kept pace, not moving closer or farther away. It would have been a good thing, save for one problem. We were moving faster than any storm this size should have been able to go, and we were still accelerating.

It wasn't natural. It couldn't be. It looked like the captain had the same concern, and he was busy reloading the harpoon cannon. Whatever came, we'd have to be ready.

And then, as suddenly as it came, the storm began to break down, until it was gone entirely. Everyone stared at the clear sky and calm waves in stunned silence.

"We… we beat it," I said.

The captain grinned. "That we did, laddie."

A ragged cheer rose up from the crew. We'd just successfully outran one of the biggest storms anyone had ever seen.

And then the sky above us darkened. Clouds materialized out of *nothing*, pouring down a deluge of water and lightning. A bolt struck our ship like a hammer from out of the skies, setting the deck ablaze. The captain swore and leaped down to order the crew, leaving me alone at the cannon.

That was when *it* appeared. A colossal dragon's head rose from the ocean, its movement displacing enough water to nearly send our ship flying. It towered over us like a tree would an ant, a dozen glowing eyes fixated only on us.

Then it *roared*; a shockwave that shattered glass, splintered wood, and twisted steel.

Stormheart, Scourge of the Seas, had arrived, ready to destroy us for encroaching upon its waters. It opened its maw, and dozens of crackling arcs of electricity rushed out to explode against the side of our ship. I tore my eyes away from the scene, and focused on aiming the cannon. There was nothing but me and the dragon, nothing to distract me. I pretended that I didn't see the flames. I pretended that I couldn't hear the screams of my crewmates, of the people that I had known for over a decade. I pretended that the heat wasn't scorching my arms, that the smoke wasn't eating at my skin.

Only me, only the beast. Inhale. Exhale. Fire.

The lance of steel tore away at a blinding speed, and there was nothing left for me to do but pray. The harpoon pierced the dragon's eye, and it *screeched.* Nothing like the roar that came before, not to show dominance or to attack, but a primal exclamation of pain that was strong enough to blow men off their feet and throw me over the side of the ship.

The last I saw before darkness took me was the deep blue of the ocean's waters.

* * *

I woke to the sound of birds crying out above me, and the sight of the captain, bleeding and burnt. The clouds had parted, leaving only clear sky, the sun shrinking into the horizon. I sat up, pain shooting down my back. We were floating on a lifeboat, our ship nowhere to be seen. I squinted into the distance. No sign of the rest of the crew.

"Cap'n…" I called out.

He stared at me, before erupting into a fit of coughs. "I can't be the captain if there's no ship for me to be the captain of."

I stared at him for a moment. "What… what happened? Where is everyone? I don't understand. Where are *we*?"

"Lifeboat," he said. I just stared at him, deadpan. He chuckled and coughed. Blood came out. "Caught you… as you were sinkin'. Dragged you onto here."

"And the others?"

"Dead." He sighed. "Or missing, but that's as good as dead out here."

So that was it then. I scanned the sea, the ocean waves gently rocking the boat. It was hard to imagine that mere minutes ago, these same waters were dragging me below. That all my friends, all the people I'd known for so long, could be gone in a single moment. Some tears rose, but I forced them down again. "Where to now, Cap'n?" I asked.

"Stop… calling me that." He wheezed. "I'm not your captain anymore. Just your dad." His breath came out ragged and weak. No. Not weak. The captain was never weak.

That was the first time he ever called me his son.

He smiled. A thin smile, but unmistakable. "This sea breeze… lovely. Good place to die." He took another breath.

"You can't die." I crawled over to him. The pain was excruciating.

"No choice in the matter." He coughed again and clenched at his chest. He wiped his face, his sleeve covered in blood.

"Capt—"

He shook his head, seemingly unable to speak.

I reached for his hand. "We're heading home then, huh, Dad?" His arm went limp. His breathing quickened, he gasped, then stopped.

I couldn't stop the tears now. I was alone. What would the captain do? What would Dad do?

"That's it then, huh?" I clenched the oars. "I'll… I'll make you proud, Dad. Count on it, alright?" With that, I rowed onward away from the setting sun, towards home. The birds had stopped calling, and only the whistle of the wind and the gentle splashes of the waves graced my ears.

Myosotis

by Jacqueline Truong

This world is one of solitude,
of endless shades of blue
never to touch each other.

My heart aches to lament, but
you grow ever further away—

But maybe, through these eyes
clouded by tears,
our colors will blur into one.

No promise of gazes exchanged,
nor any vow of brushing fingertips—

Only a fleeting dream
in which you never forgot
the feeling of my warmth.

Portrait of Madame X

Inspired by the painting "Portrait of Madame X" by John Singer Sargent, 1884

by Maria Tran

There she stands
Tall, elegant, and long
Her hair hints a reddish hue
Skin as white as snow, as if
she had always been cold
Blush creeps up her ears
Her nose stands high
Shaped by the goddesses
that reside in the sky
Madame X,
What is it like to be
the definition of beauty?
That, I will never know
Jealousy, perhaps, is my civil duty

FIREWORKS

by Elaine Lam

I reached for the flickering embers,
Sparkling fire and silver blue stars.
Though the dark hid what they were,
I felt bursts inside my chest
And I wished, deep within,
That they belonged to me.

The Ocean

by Hailey Zuniga

Ocean

Endless, Majestic

Crashing, Soothing, Moving

Fish, Dolphins, Whales, Sharks

Expanding, Astonishing, Captivating

Beautiful, Alarming

Sea

Water vs Fire

by Hailey Zuniga

Water

Calm, Steady

Waving, Swaying, Enchanting

Life, Creation, Death, Destruction

Burning, Melting, Imposing

Bright, Dangerous

Fire

ABLAZE

Inspired by the painting "Stacks, End of Summer" by Claude Monet, 1891

by Cecilia Dinh

The grass lays silent
Fiery beams burn my eyes
Birds have all gone quiet
As the searing temperature rises

Water seeps through my cracked hands
Dripping onto the scorched ground
Steam hisses from the arid land
Water is nowhere to be found

The last harvest is scarce
One piece of wheat each
Farmland turned coarse
At last it is time to leave

RIVERS, PONDS, OCEAN, EARTH

by Khanhlam Doan

River

Narrow, Swift

Rushing, Flowing, Running

Rapids, Deltas, Pebbles, Cattails

Rippling, Reflecting, Shimmering

Calm, Serene

Pond

Ocean

Restless, Vast

Crashing, Surging, Foaming

Waves, Reefs, Mountains, Trees

Growing, Producing, Sustaining

Changing, Destroying

Earth

Rain

by Hillary Nguyen

Clear, transparent curtains descend
Washing dirt from the cement
Carrying leaves away in a current
Masking the scent of a dead dove
The rain washes over me
And I'd like to think that
It washed away the dirt and stains
Scrubbed away the scent of regret
And I was made anew
But I haven't changed at all
The silent numbness in my head
Drowns out the pelting drops
That fall above and around

SECRETS

by Bethanie Luu

Let it freeze over,
Let the secrets
Be buried
In the moonlit snow
Let it sink
And let it drown
In the cold,
Murky waters.
Let the dead
Bury the dead
And shall it be
Forgotten for
All of eternity.
Let it never see
The light of day
Once more.
My toes are frozen
My limbs are cold
But together we die
For this story
To never be retold.

Loss

by Maria Tran

and there you lay
out of breath.
effortlessly,
beautifully,
enchantingly so.
but that was your last
before I had to let you go.

IN MEMORY

by Jacqueline Truong

I woke to the cry of victory;
to the smell of blood, to smoke.
Allies called my name,
but I called for yours.

Beside your lifeless body,
triumph lost all meaning.
After all, what meaning is there
in a life without you, my love?

You had made the warrior in me
yearn for the first time.
You had made me dream of grandeur,
of peace, for the first time.

I would give so much just to be
a body sleeping by your side.
To be a memory of this battlefield
and not its hero.

DOZING

by Michelle Nguyen

Dreams
Adventurous, Pleasant,
Comforting, Longing, Mesmerizing
Happiness, Memories, Insomnia, Scars
Frightening, Traumatizing, Shivering
Dark, Disastrous
Nightmares

BURNOUT

by Michelle Nguyen

Stress
Impatient, Moody
Draining, Straining, Worrying
Deadlines, Dates, Schedules, Time
Dreading, Delaying, Yielding
Apathetic, Unresponsive
Anxiety

Pleasant Desolation

by Vi Bui

Among the empty, dead silence,
Buildings that once stood so proud
Crumble into the dust that remains
Dormant until my feet kick them up.

Eerie quiet fills the air, but I can't bring myself to
Fear the noiseless nothing that lies ahead,
Growing ever further as I trail the beaten path.

However desolate the land may be,
I never feel quite so alone.
Just the pleasant emptiness I find myself in,
Keeping my senses numb and calm.

Love of the night, adoration of the
Moonlit sky that guides my way.
Now enraptured in its dark embrace,
Oh, how the cold comforts my senses.

People fear isolation, but I find it
Quaint as an empty, aging cottage
Remaining lifeless in my presence.

Still, I keep my smile as
There's joy to be found when no one's around.

Unknown treasures hidden deep within
Vacant space leaves me with more
When there's no one else to consider.

Xing paths that no one dares to tread.
You may find yourself
Zealous in the dark, at peace all alone.

Seasonal Stress

By Vi Bui

"CARLY, YOU DOWN HERE?" Lisa asked as she clambered down the basement steps, a mug in each hand. She peered over the sea of packing envelopes, tape, stickers, and more to find her partner nestled neatly in the midst of the mess.

"I haven't gone anywhere," Carly said as she added a sticker to the package in her hand. She glanced up. "Is that hot cocoa? I could really use some right now."

"Of course it is. It's like negative two degrees down here. Don't want you becoming a snowman, now do we?" Lisa smiled as she tip-toed across the paper littering the floor, careful not to disturb any packages or letters. Despite her efforts, a crinkle sounded out, a very loud one at that. "Sorry, darling. Was that one important?"

"Yeah, but I can straighten it out before it gets shipped. Or blame it on the postal service." Carly pushed aside a few plastic bins jam-packed with other supplies, revealing a lovely red rug underneath. She patted the open spot. "Right here, it's about the only place I can squeeze you in since, well…" She gestured to the army of enamel pins that conquered their couch, armed with metal pokers to defend their territory.

"How many orders did you get?" Lisa crouched down balancing the mugs. "This is way more than usual."

"Right? I didn't think I'd get so many orders so soon. My hands feel like they're about to die from frostbite." She reached out for her hot cocoa.

Lisa pulled away. "Did your tongue freeze off, too? Magic words, Mrs. No-Manners."

"Lisa, I've been working all day. Give me a break… please."

"See, was that so hard?" She handed over the cup. "Now you'd better enjoy that. It's my special mix, full of calories and sugar."

Carly looked down at the sweet concoction then shrugged and took a sip. "Calories don't count on Christmas anyways."

"It's only the fourth."

"Target sells decorations in November. Your point?"

"They don't decide when the holidays are." Lisa rolled her eyes. "Though that's not going to stop me from getting in the spirit of things."

"Well, that's not going to stop me from drinking this either." Carly took a gulp. "Gosh I needed this. I'm so tired."

"So, how close are you to being done?"

Carly hung her head and laughed weakly. "This is just a quarter of the orders that I have to wrap. And this doesn't even count incoming orders. You know there's always last minute stragglers." She held out her fingers and showed them to her partner, their tips tinged pink from pinching paper.

"Oh, goodness." Lisa glanced around the basement. Countless piles of manila envelopes obscured the red rug and the walls. She scooted closer to Carly and leaned on her arm. "I know you're stubborn about things like this, but you know I'm always here to help, right?"

Carly sighed. "I'm fine, really. I'm just complaining, but this is nothing. I could go all day if I had to."

"You already have."

Carly pulled away. "What do you mean? I started working around four and it's—"

"It's eleven. When was the last time you looked outside?"

"Oh." Carly rubbed the back of her neck as she looked out the small window, at the darkening sky. She rose slowly, her back cracking and popping from disuse as she stretched out her weary limbs. "That doesn't sound good."

"You think?" Lisa said. "What about those yoga poses I taught you? Breaks? Anything?"

"I don't need that. I just push through the day to day. I can handle it."

"I'm just saying, this work routine isn't healthy, and I care about you. I can't help but worry."

"I know, but I just want to get these orders out on time and I don't want to get backed up so…" She looked over the supplies scattered across the room, her work consuming most of the tables and chairs. Her eyes fell on Lisa, who sat with weary eyes amidst the clutter threatening to engulf her. "I guess I could take a break for today."

"Carly…"

"For a few days, then. We can call it a mini-vacation or something."

"Just what I was thinking. Now come here." Lisa opened up her arms. Carly didn't hesitate to plop herself on the plush rug and toss herself into them. The warmth that radiated from Lisa's smile made the seasonal chill seem so far away. "You don't need me to keep telling you to rest, Carly. Your body already does."

"I know, but it's hard for me. I feel—I don't know—wasteful? Yeah, wasteful with my time and your time and—"

She felt a finger touch her lips. "No more of that. Let's just rest up. It's Christmas, after all."

"It's the fourth."

"And yet when I go to Target, what do I see?" Lisa smiled as she hugged Carly tighter.

THE DRUMMER IN NEW YORK

by Christopher Nguyen

There was a skillful drummer in New York
Who loved to play songs with his fork
Crowds would hear his sick beats
They'd stay so long they'd bring sheets
And he turned out to be a small stork

Making a Dictionary

by Vi Bui

How many definitions can a word have?
Two or three or four or more
Crane or Bark or Clip or Bow
We're used to it by now

How many times have we defined love?
In words, in songs, in stories
On paper, in court, with people, and more
Yet how accurate are they all

Love is a feeling, Love is a word
It's something people pine for
Is everyone wrong? Is everyone right?
I ask these questions but it's not worth the fight

Love is whatever it ends up being
There are no rules, no laws, no forces, no instructions
Just you and I and whatever it comes to be
A word made for us to discover and define

It can be like a movie, magical and made up
It can be like a song, smooth and sad
It can be like a story, planned out to a T
It can be like a promise, one bound to break

Love isn't perfect and that's the funny thing
No matter how it's described it'll never quite fit
It's not science, nor witchcraft, nor anything new
Yet as we fall, it feels like the right thing to do

If love is romantic why don't we make it so
Share a drink with me, share your time
Listen to our voices ramble on and on
And see what love can do to you

Love is like sunglasses
It tints your world pink
While the word may stay the same
It makes everything sweet

Paint the world with me
Make the planet our movie set
While we craft our love story
We'll make the greatest song yet

Before Magic

by Mia Gallardo

Before magic, darkness consumed.
Before magic, life was despaired.
And magic was the medicine,
Would cure them of rot and stress,
Let them forget about the past.
Magic distorted their dark, horrific world,
Turned it bright, angelic, too alluring to depart.
Magic flowed through their blood,
Invaded every vein and cell,
Until it slithered its way to their heart
Now poisoned, perilous, and black.
But that's what they wanted,
To feel nothing.
Before magic, they felt everything.
Before magic, they felt pain.
They were fooled,
And, now, they're gone.

INSOMNIA

by Michelle Nguyen

For it gave me a new escape,
But the late nights kept changing.
The once calming night
Was then a dreaded time,
And there was no escape
That brought beauty and life
In the form of dreams.
And those restless nights,
Filled with anxious fear,
Held me frozen in time.

Red

by Hillary Nguyen

BREATHE IN. BREATHE OUT. Red tried to slow his breaths, or at least muffle them. His shoulders shook as he covered his mouth. He couldn't let them find him.

It was dark inside the hollow core of the tree trunk, and the only light source was a sharp ray of light piercing through a small knothole, his only window outside. Maybe this giant oak tree would be his salvation, or the cause of his death if he were caught. He hoped that the scent of leaves and dirt would cover his scent from the Wolves.

Red's back was against the bark walls of the circular hideaway and his knees tucked close to his chest. He had barely squeezed through a narrow opening between the roots, the only exit. At least he wasn't claustrophobic. He looked at the muddy forest beyond the small opening then glanced at the wretched, wooden picnic basket next to him, his village's annual offering to the Witches.

He grimaced, and his hand twitched with the urge to hurl that dead weight, but the village would kill him if he failed to deliver the basket—not that he'd be alive if he succeeded. No matter where he turned, there would always be death at the end.

He'd prefer it at the hands of other humans than a Wolf's though. Humans wouldn't tear him apart or eat him alive.

A couple more minutes. He'd wait a couple more minutes before leaving the tree's shelter. From just beyond the tree, a growl sounded.

Someone or something sniffed the air. "Close," a gravelly voice murmured.

Red's whole body shook. His heart thumped, and he inhaled, clutching at his chest. The Wolves. They had found him.

A pause outside. Footsteps came closer. Red reached into the basket, praying that the villagers had packed a knife.

"Ash," another voice whined, "they won't let me play with them."

"Not right now, Silver. Go play with mud or something," Ash said. He had to be mere inches from the knothole opening.

"Ugh, seriously? I'm not five."

Red stifled his mouth as the Wolf, Ash, turned away from the tree.

Red could imagine a younger Wolf pouting at the larger one. The voices kept going back and forth until Ash left, sounding irritated. Red sat still, waiting for the other pair of feet to retreat. He widened his eyes when a face peeked into the knothole.

"You're the one he's been chasing? You barely have any meat on you."

Red froze, his heartbeat quickening.

The Wolf frowned. "Just come out."

With no response, the Wolf narrowed his eyes. "What, did you want my brother? I'll call Ash back." He inhaled a deep breath into his lungs and cupped his hands around his mouth.

"No, wait. I'll come out." Red scrambled to his feet, grabbed the basket, and crawled out into the chilly evening. One Wolf was already bad enough.

The Wolf smiled. "I'm Silver. Your name?"

"Scarlet."

Silver turned away and cupped his hands around his mouth again. "A—"

"Red! It's Red."

Silver lowered his hands. "No point lying to a Wolf, dummy."

Red stayed quiet as he looked at his surroundings from the corner of his eyes—no boughs or branches lying on the ground that he could use, not that they'd do much damage. As for Silver… even the younger Wolf had a muscular physique. Red winced at the thought of being pinned down while trying to escape.

Silver smirked and motioned to his right. "Might as well gain some distance from him, right?"

Red warily eyed him and followed. Maybe—

"You better not bolt," Silver said, a hand shifting to a claw.

Red looked away. A still lake lay in front of them, and he watched as a speckled stone skipped across the surface, leaving ripples in its path. He looked to his side, to Silver who was holding out another stone. "Wanna try?"

Red hesitated for a second before grabbing the smooth round pebble and hurling it. It made it a couple feet out before sinking.

Silver snickered. "You suck." He reached for more pebbles and skipped them across the lake with a flick of a wrist.

Red glowered and sat down, dropping the basket with a loud thud. He rummaged through it. No knives or anything sharp he could use. Only some food, a bottle, and a voodoo doll. Red swore at the village in his head as he took a wrapped sandwich out.

Who cares. They wouldn't know, and besides, his stomach was screaming at him. He bit a large chunk off.

Something slimy squirmed against his tongue. He gagged and spat it out, watching as a worm plopped onto the dirt and wriggled towards freedom. Red threw the rest of the sandwich into the lake.

Of course those cursed Witches ate worms for lunch. He crouched closer to the lake and cupped some water into his hands to rinse away the lingering taste.

Silver sat next to him, a hand propping his chin up. "What a waste of food." He glanced at the basket. "What else you got in there?"

Red wiped his mouth with the back of a hand and turned to Silver. "More disgusting food. A glass bottle of apple cider. And…" He reached into the basket and pulled out a little voodoo doll of himself. He sneered at it. "And me, the newest sacrifice for some bloody ritual."

"Your village sent you to the Witches? Your family's gotta be devastated."

Red scoffed. "They're the ones who sent me off. Needed to pay off their debt."

"Oh… sorry."

"That's just how it is." Red looked down. "Why'd you even bring me here? To kill me after I got a little bit of hope?" He slumped onto the ground and pulled out a blade of grass.

"That wouldn't be fun at all."

"So I'm a toy. Great." Red lay down on the grass, his eyes to the sky. He always seemed to be living due to someone else's whims, only ever given the bare necessities for a healthy body to please the Witches. They'd probably love to dissect him and see his heart, but for now, he was a form of entertainment for a bored Wolf.

"No, no, it's not that." Silver furrowed his eyebrows. "It's just… the other Wolves always leave me out of everything. I have Ash but he's busy hunting for our food, and, well, I thought it might be nice to talk to someone else."

"I guess." Red snorted. The first decent conversation he had in years and it was with a Wolf, the very being the village had always threatened to throw him to if he acted out. "Not like I'll be here for long though. A sacrifice for the Witches and all."

"Then just don't go."

"Are you serious? The village will hunt me down. They can't just stop supplying the Witches."

Silver raised an eyebrow. "A few humans aren't hard to deal with—"

A rustle; a snap of a twig. Red scrambled up. A man swore as he limped out of the brush, claw marks fresh on his cheek and clothes.

He glared at Red. "Finally found you, you stupid brat. Hurry up and come with me."

Red stood firm.

The man—Greg, Red wasn't sure but he couldn't care less—scowled. "What, not even a day out of our sight, and you got it in your head that you deserve to live?"

Red clenched his fists.

"Oh, you're serious?" Greg sneered. "A bird peck would hurt me more than your hits. Or you gonna use that runt behind you like a little baby?"

Silver bared his teeth, his fingers extending into claws. Red shook his head at him and took the cider bottle out of the basket. This wasn't a Wolf's battle. "I don't need him to finish you off."

Greg lunged, but missed as Red sidestepped and swung his basket. A wooden crunch sounded as it rammed into Greg's head.

The villager cursed under his breath, a hand to his injury. He punched Red in the gut, sending him towards a tree gasping for breath.

Red smashed the bottle against the trunk, and he felt its contents flowing down his hand into a puddle. As Greg charged, Red swung the jagged end at the back of Greg's head.

Greg winced and pulled his arm back, only for a rock to be hurled into his face by Silver.

Now was Red's chance. He tripped Greg while his eyes were on the Wolf. Silver pounced and pinned him to the ground.

Red slashed Greg's throat, forming a thin line of blood before he jammed the bottle in. The body stopped struggling.

Red's hands shook and his heart pounded as he backed away. "I actually did it." He covered his mouth. The taste of iron stung his tongue. Blood pricked from little cuts on his fingers. Red tore off a part of his cloak and wrapped it around his hands.

Silver stared at the body. "Didn't know you had it in you. Ash'll probably let you off now, seeing as there's a perfectly good meal right here."

Red turned away. Aside from his wild heart, a gnawing numbness spread throughout his body—was he supposed to feel something more? Red took deep breaths, in and out. He looked back at Silver. "How likely is it that I can stay with you and not get eaten?"

"I'll figure it out, I'm sure I can convince the other Wolves." Silver smirked. "You could help us to bait more villagers."

Red nodded; he was alive. No, more than that—for once, he felt free. And he wanted to keep it that way. Forget his family and the village and the Witches.

He'd live for himself.

Motivation

by Vinh Park

Thrown into a labyrinth of dead ends,
you feel like escape is around the corner,
But every time you expect a path,
you encounter a wall of Writer's Block.
You want to sit in a corner and give up,
but the Deadline dogs sniff at your trail—
You must continue.
Armed with the sword of Inspiration,
and the shield of Determination,
slash past ghouls of Distraction,
trudge in swamps of Boredom,
blaze through jungles of Hopelessness,
guided by the light of Motivation
until you reach Completion.

Writing a Storm

by Vincent Quach

A day in the creative writing class
Where artistry shines brightly like glass.
Pencils dance as they write
On paper from left to right,
To create a story for today's task.

Let's write down our best thoughts.
Many can be the best in the lot.
In the journal it holds,
Your stories to be told.
There's always one with a twisted plot.

Just Have Fun with It

by Brian Ly

Another alphabet poem to write.

Barf out words as you please,
Create a mess if you'd like:
Dog, cat, refrigerator.
Even that will work fine
For creative liberty allows it.

Give it half of your all,
Horrendous it may be, but
It'll give a good laugh,
Justified in a great way.

Kale is a filler word,
Let's move on to the next line.

Make a poem nonsensical.
No one can complain if
One or two lines are off
as Purposely, they are.

Queer that may sound
Riveting it may be
Stupid, most definitely,
Though stupid is filled with glee.

Understand that I'm out of ideas.

Very quickly

Will this poem lose its

Xany charm (and rhythm)

Yet I doubt it ever had any.

Zoo.

WISH A LITTLE

by Jasmine Bui

I see the world with rose-colored shades,
And wish on stars and birthday cakes.
And yes, I'm the person who plays that charade,
Because even if I cry, my tears will one day fade.

But why now are dandelions so hard to find?
Is it the fault of those who left this world behind?
Or maybe because no one is left to remind
That your childhood isn't something to confine.

Do people still throw coins in fountains?
With hopes as high as the tallest mountains?
A person who finds themselves trapped, surrounded,
Is a person who sees the future unfounded.

Can people accept that their dreams,
Are more than just a big scheme?
It may not be to an extreme,
But a dream is a dream
And that's all you need.

I wish people weren't so wistful
And would listen, plain and simple:
Wish a little.

A Green World

by Khanh Tran

Color fills flowers.
In the backdrop are the trees
With one color: Green.

Nature's Aviators

by Khanh Tran

Soaring through the skies,
White doves flock elegantly.
Like angels, they fly.

Springful Days

by Khanh Tran

The sky daubed with white
Illuminates the green grass
While the sun shines bright.

Dandelion

by An Huynh

A wisp in the wind,
A presence small yet cherished
By all who pass by

Forget Me Not

by An Huynh

Dreadful it is that
Your petals have been plucked out
For a pointless game

Nymphaea

by An Huynh

Elegant and bright,
A beauty so alluring
Yet unreachable

Spring Things

by Vincent Quach

Spring Greens

The leaves begin green.
And out grows the soft green grass.
A green spring has come.

Flowers

Here come the new buds.
Sprout from the dirt as they bloom.
They show their beauty.

Trees

Reaching to the sky.
Branches grasping at the clouds.
Leaves covering all.

Spring's Arrival

by Hillary Nguyen

The snow has melted.
Pretty flowers sprout and grow.
Dwell in the moment.

Weeds

by Hillary Nguyen

Sprouting in the cracks.
Trampled and yanked but they grow.
Always remain strong.

River

by Hillary Nguyen

A rushing current.
Traveling through the terrain.
The fish swim along.

Melodic Memory

by Kayla Nguyen

A bird's melody
grows quiet as seasons change.
Lovely, but soon fades.

Sunrise

by Kayla Nguyen

Dawn brings gentle light
that warms the body and mind,
starting a new day.

Raining Flowers

by Kayla Nguyen

A falling flower,
dancing gently in the breeze,
settles on the grass.

COVID

by Christopher Nguyen

Virus spreading fast
Coughing around the planet
Wash your dirty hands

BEACH DAYS

by Christopher Nguyen

Sand touching moist feet
Beach Balls take off like seagulls
Sun shining on waves

CHRISTMAS

by Christopher Nguyen

Reindeer on rooftop
Hot chocolate near fire
Christmas lights shine bright

SOULS

by Mia Gallardo

In the dead of night
Our cold bodies are taken,
But our souls ignite

SPRING

by Mia Gallardo

The sun glistening,
Giving warmth to our bodies
As flowers blossom

WAR

by Mia Gallardo

A forthcoming war,
Chaotic, yet beautiful,
Shows that life is short

Sea

by Bryce Le

Deep cobalt waters
Hiding a vibrant seascape
Under crashing waves

Sky

by Bryce Le

A calm, silent breeze
Carries clouds on their journey
Through the azure sky

Stars

by Bryce Le

In the vast expanse
A million glimmering lights
Shine down upon Earth

Frogs

by An Huynh

Tiny green creatures
Of happiness hop around,
Lighting up the town.

Stars & Moon

by An Huynh

Lanterns of the night
Guide us forth toward a path
That we hope will last

Meadows

by An Huynh

Spacious quiet fields
To lay beside the flowers
And rest weary eyes

Elemental Poetry

by Stella Nguyen

The Moon

The night sky lights up
We are blessed by her smile
Her beauty gives life

The Sun

She gives us purpose
We dance to the light of dawn
While her glow shines down

The Gift of Fire

Burning with passion
As fierce as a blazing sword
She grants us her life

Wind's Dance

A playful spirit
She sings with powerful blows
Guiding us to peace

Koi Fish

by Khanhlam Doan

Scales slipping through streams
White tail flashing through ripples
Mouth gaping above

Geode

by Khanhlam Doan

Rough shell lined with cracks
Hides rows of shining crystals
Hollow surprises

Moon

by Khanhlam Doan

Silver sphere looks down
Specked with craters, it orbits
One flag waves alone

THE SEASONS

by Cecilia Dinh

THE GROWTH

Tiny at the start

Blooming with a blissful burst

Filling fields with life

TRICKLE, TRICKLE

Through the air it falls

Flowing down the window next

To the ground it seeps

FOLLOW AHEAD

Frigid air whispers

Crisp leaves crunch under my feet

Bare the path ahead

GONE WITH FLAMES

Fiery beams shine down

Scorching the frail things below

Until none are left

THE SEASONS

Scorching heat lays calm

Delicate petals, dull leaves

White dust in our palms

I Walk at Dawn

by Brandon Nguyen

And here marks their place.
They lived, they ran, 'til sunset,
So now, I may walk.

In Normandy

by Brandon Nguyen

Here grow five poppies.
Who planted them, we won't know.
Yet here they still grow.

A Legacy Passes

by Brandon Nguyen

If I pass my torch,
The one I once was given,
May you hold it too.

INNER STRENGTH

by Kaitlyn Truong

Tears are trivial
Change is unattainable
Only if you cave

RAIN SUMMONS THE OLD CAT

By Kayla Nguyen

Plant pot sat under the awning.
Old cat laid in that pot, yawning
as the rain fell.
Poor plant crushed,
crumbled into dust.
But we greet the cat, we wish it well.

Plant pot sat under the awning.
No old cat in that pot, yawning
as the rain still fell.
Plant untouched,
sprouting in a rush.
Old cat gone, we say our farewell.

The Wilted Rose

by Stella Nguyen

Your leaves wilt beneath my gentle touch
And your shriveled petals reveal your sad song
I kneel and caress your fragile thorns
They pick at me as I care for you with bare hands
I hold you close and whisper a promise
I will shelter you from the strong rain's scorn
I will be there to catch your fall
To nurture this wounded rose
Until once again,
Her stem stands tall

Fox and the Sour Grapes

by Elaine Lam

I noticed a tall tree
With ripe violet grapes
And tried my very best
To reach its high branches.
But I lacked the strength
In my tiny little legs,
And my straining neck
Was far too short.
Still I looked up, hoping
One would fall on its own
But tired and frustrated,
I retreated home.
It's not that I wasn't hungry
It's not that they would be sour
It's just that there would never be
Someone willing to pick them for me.

Years that Fly By

by Hailey Zuniga

Childhood

Happy, Peaceful

Laughing, Jumping, Exploring

Youth, Nonage, Maturity, Adultness

Aging, Paying, Working

Older, Wiser

Adulthood

Good Morning, Good Night

by Hailey Zuniga

Morning

Cold, Frosty

Freezing, Brightening, Waking

Sunrise, First Light, Sunset, Dead of Night

Darkening, Sleeping, Dreaming

Dimness, Gloom

Night

Blossoming Memorial

by **Keanu Hua**

Amaryllis, sparkling red and standing proud
Buttercup, growing close and up to your chin
Cattleya, gracing the mind on the windowsill
Daffodil, pushing us towards the beyond
Evening primrose, recalling a romantic scene
Forget-Me-Not, promising your eternity
Gardenia, concealing a forgotten purity
Hibiscus, beauty here for only a moment
Iris, our trusted, our protector
Jasmine, climbing silently, aroma flooding
Kniphofia, rising high and burning low
Lycoris, shedding its leaves and blossoming alone
Marigold, a golden firework, bursting, shimmering, gone
Narcissus, resurrecting the dead marigold soul
Orchid, a column of royals atop a spire of green
Peony, a noble medicine hidden within a bush
Quince, red fortune and a thousand at once
Rose, thorns protecting a multitude of color
Snapdragon, soaring to the skies with a vow of truth
Tulip, perfectly modest grace, mistaken for exceptional grandeur
Ulex, gleaming golden in all weather
Violet, shrinking away, hiding away, loving away
Wisteria, an ancient spreading across eternity
Xanthisma, flourishing in the desert dryness
Yarrow, mending broken souls and hearts
Zinnia, forever an ally despite it all

The Last Time

by Keanu Hua

SNIP.

MORRIS HELD THE bird-of-paradise up to the garden lights, examining the vibrant green stem and the orange-sunset crown of flowers at the top. Outside, the wind and rain battered the glass roof and brick walls, but inside, there was only the flutter of butterflies, the buzz of bees, the prowl of wasps. The night had long since swallowed the day and the fierce storm would have made for lovely ambience for rest, but still, Morris had energy to spare. His mother had retired to bed early, yet it would be much longer before his youthful vigor of sixteen years ran dry.

He took out a lacquer wood tray and filled it with a shallow layer of water, watching as the ripples ran outward. Then, he grabbed a handful of black, polished stones from the bag next to him, dropping them into the tray as a circle, and setting the bird-of-paradise in the middle of the tray, in a small square of substrate.

"That should do it." He marched over to one of the tables and set it down among the other projects. It was much simpler than them, what with their multi-leaved, multi-flower bouquets, but that bird-of-paradise crown amidst the brown and black was all the color and detail it needed.

Morris paused. Plucking a few leaves from a small bush at the side, he pushed them into the soil next to the flower. "Now, that should do it."

He stretched as he sauntered out of the garden section to the front desk of the store, aimlessly spinning as he walked, but still weaving in between the tables, the projects, the flowers, the vases. Then, he pulled aside the blinds; Mother had told him to set sandbags out front, but how deep could the water possibly be?

There was a boy around his age on the opposite side of the street, dancing feverishly in the rain with neither coat nor shoes, as though forced to perform some ritual in order to live. He looked familiar, but no matter how much Morris wracked his brain, only the faint memory of someone crying came to mind. That someone in his memories had a flower crown, but the boy dancing out there only had a single flower.

It was mesmerizing. Morris had never seen someone move with such desperation—or was it hope? A dying man, hearing of his salvation and throwing himself around in joy? Or a despairing man, hearing of his execution and hurling himself in agony? Whatever it was, the boy thrashed backwards and forward, every individual part of his body under the control of his fervor, dancing to some unseen rhythm, some unheard song.

Part of him felt that he and the boy were the same in age, but the dancing boy looked like he could be an equal to professionals.

He danced as though his entire life depended on it. And hand reaching towards the sky, he collapsed into the shallow water.

"Oh no." Morris put on his raincoat and zipped it up while shoving on his rain boots, hurrying outside as the rain and wind shoved him into the door.

Distantly, a ship's bell tolled by the roiling coast.

"Hey!" The boom of thunder was his reply. He ran out into the street, gritting his teeth as his heavy footsteps sent the frigid water onto his jeans, while the wind bit at his arms.

Once he was next to the boy, Morris grabbed him from under his arms, dragging him towards the store. "Thank God you're light," he muttered.

Morris maintained a brisk pace backwards, trained by years of hauling soil and fertilizer. He headed up the steps through the front door and set the boy down on a chair in a little corner where four garden plots made a crossroads.

Morris took off his soaked raincoat and muddy boots. He pushed his hand against the boy's forehead. Cold and clammy. Morris hurried into a backroom and took out a can of tomato soup, dumped it into a bowl from a nearby cabinet, and shoved it into the microwave. Grabbing a pile of towels from another cabinet, he hurried back and placed them onto the stone edge of a nearby garden plot.

He grabbed a soft cloth and rubbed it over the boy's head, then turned it over to dry his arms.

"Ah, Morris..." The boy's arm snaked out of his grasp, his eyes fluttered open, and a grin formed.

Had he met him before? Morris noticed his guest's pallor, highlighted only by the pale-yellow daffodil in his hair. His eyes, clothing, everything was gray, as though someone had drained the boy of color.

"Do... do I know you?" Morris asked. A slow nod, like a king offering his judgment. Morris stepped back. "Who—"

The boy's grin turned to a frown. "You've forgotten me, haven't you?" He tilted his head. "But maybe it's better this way." He rose, stumbled, fell.

Morris caught him, swallowing nervously. "So then, who are you?" He set the boy back onto the chair.

Another head tilt. Another grin.

"Your best friend." A pause as the boy inhaled, bit his lip, exhaled. "The one who promised to always be there for you. The one who said he loved you. The one who you must've forgotten all about." His hand drifted over to his black hair. "I'm Louis. Here." He grabbed his daffodil, offering it to Morris. "Smell it. You'll remember."

Morris obliged.

The daffodils in bloom in a nearby planter. A blushing boy in an argyle sweater, refusing to face him. A flower crown: a bird-of-paradise blazing glory, a flame lily red claw, a white rose gleaming. A daffodil.

A vague promise from Morris. A disappointed "oh" from Louis.

The scurrying of someone else—someone who shouldn't have been there.

The memory ended.

Morris stared up at the fading smile of his former friend. "How did I—"

"You were busy. Busy taking care of yourself, your studies, your trumpet lessons, your gardening." Louis rested his head on his fist, leaning forward. "Can't blame you. We got different classes, no time to hang out after school because you wanted to be the top of the top. Then, I moved away, 'cause I was sick, and I guess, needing to handle all that you were going through, your mind needed to make some space. So then, I was gone." He flicked his other hand into the air, as though dispersing dust.

Meanwhile, discomfort gripped at Morris, like a bramble of fig suffocating a tree. "Sick with what?" He gulped.

The other boy smiled weakly. "Lovesickness. Maybe it's hard for someone like you to wrap your head around, but…" He chuckled. "That wasn't the case for my family. Said I was sick to love someone like you. That's why they took me away."

Silence. Morris was left slack-mouthed at the revelation. All those years ago, back in middle school, when he started to realize that even his brilliance had limits. All those years ago, when he refused to accept it. All those years ago, when he pushed himself to the brink.

So many bleary-eyed days, crying from stress, nobody there to comfort him, now misty moments in his hole-filled memories. He vaguely recalled high test scores, but no happiness. Only a sense of relief, swallowed soon after by his unsatisfied ambition. He kept moving forward, each and every day, forgetting all about the present.

Where were his friends back then? He remembered a few memories of enjoyment with them, but everything was wreathed in the anxiety of his desires, like a dying lycoris alone in an island of lotuses. It felt like all he could remember was all that he had experienced. If even his friends back then could barely be recalled, no wonder someone who vanished was all but gone.

Morris blinked. "I… I don't know what to say."

"Neither do I. I never thought that we'd meet again, but look at us now."

Louis looked over at the projects, at the flower arrangements that Morris had spent the night making.

Beep. Both boys turned to the backroom, and Morris got up, returning with a bowl of tomato soup and a spoon. He pushed one of the tables over, setting it and the bowl in front of his former friend who smiled.

"I think I could've lived the rest of my life without meeting you again. Maybe that would've been better." Louis stared down at the bowl and aimlessly swirled the soup inside. "I tried to forget all the regrets and pains back then, but no matter how hard I tried, you always came back. I wondered how you were doing, 'cause last I saw you, you were in so much pain. Nothing satisfied you—swallowed up by your relentless want for achievement." He looked away. "I wanted to be there for you, but my parents didn't let me. Thought you must've been the reason I got sick, I guess. Maybe they're right."

A weak chuckle, then a sip of the soup. "But even if I'm sick, it would've been fine to me. They didn't see it that way, though, so we moved away, far from you." He looked upwards. "But I still kept you in my heart, through it all, no matter how much they told me it was wrong. I felt like if I died or forgot about you, you would die."

"I never got that bad, no."

"Well," Louis said, "I think I prefer it that way. Means we aren't as linked as I thought. You know, I used to fantasize about meeting you again, and now? I could cease to be, and I think, after seeing you in front of me, that'd be fine." A blue morpho butterfly landed next to him, and he watched as it opened and closed its wings.

"Oh," Morris said. "Uh, please don't—not in front of me, or here, a—"

Louis laughed. "Still the same after all these years, eh? Still awkward. It's cute." His exuberant expression turned to a pained frown. "But it hurts. It reminds me of just how sick I am. I want to love you, but I've got no love left after the treatment. Told to hate that part of me, until it became the only thing I knew myself for. But it's funny. Do you know the three components of love?"

Morris got up, shaking his head as Louis straightened up in his seat, his arms on the chair's armrests and continued, "Treatment assumes you're only interested in one of the three, but when I told you that I loved you, I didn't care for that 'one.' I just wanted you, because… because I wanted to see you grow, I think. You tried so hard, and I loved you for that, but now, it's hard for a guy to even touch me without me freezing up and thinking of the worst possible things."

"You seemed fine with me, though?" Morris said.

"Because you're you. Even though it hurts, I don't care. I still love you too much for something like heartache to get in my way. But, I know that I can't ask you to love me." His head tilted back and forth like a doll. "You're not that way. That's fine. I can't ask anything that extreme from you, but if this is the last time I'll see you—"

"What do you mean by last time? What if—"

"Shh." Louis paused in his seat. "Don't worry so much. I just want closure, at this point, something to shut up this heartache burning in me. It's not your fault, but I do feel like." He inhaled deeply. "I feel like I'm dying. I mean not literally, but I guess having to hate myself so much, I don't feel like I'm worthy. What do I have to be proud of?"

"But you're such an amazing dancer."

A gentle laugh. "My parents don't want a dancer. They want a nice, lovely son who will have a wife, not a sick child who wants a boyfriend. But now… I just want closure. I want to know that you're content." He got up and stepped forward. "Are you?"

Morris blinked. After all those years, his life had steadied out. It wasn't easy maintaining his exemplar position, but at least he wasn't on the verge of collapse anymore, near the brink of sobbing, and he had started to reconcile with the rest of his friends, who he had forgotten about over the years.

"I think I am."

"Good, good." A few seconds of silence as Louis drank the soup. "Then, may I ask one last favor? Before I might die?" Louis looked up at Morris. "I'm joking, of course, but sometimes… sure feels like I already have. But, can we do this? A favor as two old friends having a chance meeting, a half helping a half to make two new wholes, and not as a crush?"

"I… I guess I'll say yes if it's not too much."

The other rose, shambling away from the chair, towards Morris, and reached for his wrist. "Dance with me."

"Dance?" Morris backed away. "I—I can't dance, and you said that, well, don't you think that's too much touch, if—"

"Maybe. But even if it hurts, I know I'll love it, this last time. Maybe I should've just forgotten all about the heartbreak you accidentally caused, but I can't do that. I don't want to hurt you that way, keeping you as the culprit but never offering a chance to redeem yourself." Louis tightened his grip. "I want you… I want us to know that we'll have one last, happy memory. I want to know that we're going to be okay. That's what I meant by closure. So, would you indulge me in this last request?"

Morris swallowed. "Fine." He stiffened as his former friend took us his hand and leaned into his shoulder. Morris grimaced as soaked clothing pressed against him.

"Just follow my lead. Just follow me." Louis hummed some old ballroom song for the two of them to follow, and it didn't take long before Morris no longer minded.

Where before Louis was thrashing in the rain, he was now slow and delicate, like a blooming flower. He stepped back towards the miniature cliff-garden, the one overgrown by amaryllis and white chrysanthemums, then two steps forward towards another plot filled with daffodils and forget-me-nots, shaped like a heart.

Morris glanced away, looking around the garden. Slowly, bits and pieces of memory filtered back into his mind, of a boy's birthday, wrapped in the low, sonorous timbres of an old ballroom song, lit by the aroma of daffodils, as they and the rest of their friends drifted to sleep in that bygone room. He remembered Louis taking his arm, hugging it, muttering something, some promise that was long forgotten.

Louis's breathing slowed, and more and more did Morris lead the dance, until eventually, his friend's feet stopped moving, with shallow breathing and fluttering eyes. Yet, silent as Louis was, Morris could see an unfamiliar jubilation in his sleepy expression, the bittersweet sort that a soldier's wife would give before the final battle as they danced together, one where she knew that her beloved would more likely perish than survive—yet still being thankful to have had a final dance.

Louis relaxed into his friend's shoulder and arms. "It's the last time… after all this time," he said.

With a relieved sigh, Morris set his friend back down onto a chair, handed his towels to finish drying off. Then, he plugged a little heater into an outlet, set it at Louis's feet, and picked up his bird-of-paradise project from earlier, placing it down in front of his friend, who startled at the crunch of the wood upon the wicker table.

"You're not cold, are you?" Morris asked.

He shook his head. "Actually, I feel warmer than ever."

"I… I think that's your veins constricting to retain heat. Would you like some new clothes? Or, well, feel free to shower and get changed, at this point." Morris gestured up the stairs. "I should've offered that to you earlier, but I sort of forgot, I guess."

"I think I would too if a forgotten friend suddenly showed up after dancing for thirty minutes all alone in the streets."

"That long?"

A nod. "It may be weird, but I dance my fullest when it rains, like it washes away everything, leaving just the me of so long ago. That's why I was out there, dancing. Didn't think I'd find you. Funny how fate works, huh?"

"Well." He paused. "Well, I'm happy, I—"

Louis chuckled. "Happy? Try content. I think that'd be better. Nobody's going to be happy with heartbreak." He paused to examine the bird-of-paradise, touching its leaves. "In a way you might get it: something like this got into my heart, grew and grew like a weed, split it. Then, it died. But no matter how much time passes, the cracks are still going to be there. But over time, it hurts less and less. It'll always be there, fading, fading…"

"So, will you be okay?"

Louis glanced upwards for a moment. "I think I will be. But more importantly, thanks for giving me this closure. Just dancing in your arms, feeling you, I know that I can keep going now, that I'll get better." He stumbled upward, putting his arms on the table to steady himself. "Ah, but I think I'll need you to, uh, lend me some dry clothes."

Morris offered his hand, and Louis grabbed it. "Just, as a friend, right?"

The other boy laughed. "Ah, dense as always. Of course. Nothing more, nothing less. "

Silently, Morris helped him out of the greenhouse, towards the hallway that led into the house proper.

"But," Louis continued, "this is my last day here. Maybe we'll meet again. Maybe we won't. Either way, I'll be okay."

Morris turned off the lights to the greenhouse, glancing back at the nightlights embedded in the garden plots, how the flowers and scenes were illuminated in the darkness.

Standing proudest among them was the bird-of-paradise, with a gentle hanging lamp blessing its radiant crown with a heavenly glow.

SISYPHUS

by Vinh Park

To a task unending, Zeus had me sent,
Toiling up a mountain, again and again.
Though shoving a boulder destroys my shoulders,
When I get to the top, I start all over,
As the boulder rolls back down the bend.

The Swing

Inspired by the painting "The Swing" by Jean-Honoré Fragonard, 1767

by Jasmine Bui

Hidden in a clearing of lush foliage and bright greenery,
Illuminated by the rays through the tree's welcoming arms,
Sat high above on a swing and joyous at the beautiful scenery,
Was a lady in pink with a look of alarm.

She swung forward and back,
With her arms at her side,
And her dress billowing like clouds,
Was unable to hide.

And the men, old peeping toms with grubby hands and sleazy smiles,
Reached out their long limbs in lust of her youth.
And she, as if the space between them were nothing more than mere miles,
Looked on at their desire while ignoring the truth.

She swung forward and back,
Her face to the sky,
And their calls from below
Went unreplied.

Twisting and turning, black brambles branched up with height,
Stretched tight and held low, the rope ran real tight.
The greens and the blues made it all seem unreal,

And yet the sight had a certain appeal.

And with a sudden cry, there was choking silence.
Oblivious, they didn't hear her pleas for help,
And left without seeing her timeless, lifeless.

2020(1)

by Bryce Le

We retreat to our castles
Of concrete and glass,
Hide away from the world
And wait for the end.

So much we've forgotten
As we idled, days flying by
Watching our world
Through little glass windows.

Nothing but empty streets
Wait for us outside
As our eyes stay glued to glass
Day in and day out.

And when the news would break,
We'd rise up in righteous fury
Before we'd sit down and carry on
As if nothing ever happened.

"Next year will be different," we say
But in our haste to forget
We lose the lessons we learned
And the cycle begins anew.

A new year, the same old.

The Glass Dome

by Kayla Nguyen

A gray sky looks over the city in a glass dome.
Where the people hide, afraid to roam.
Then enters the city a bard
Who comes singing stories from lands afar
And the glass dome is no longer home.

They learn of the world outside the glass
And the dome begins to crack.
Outside with the bard they follow and go
To strange new places with grand sights to show.
The world they know is no longer black.

THE FALLEN KING

Inspired by the painting "War. The Exile and the Rock Limpet"

by Joseph M.W Turner, 1842

by Khanh Tran

A lone figure stands beneath a blue sky
While the golden sun peeks from the ground.
Oh, how its colors reach so high
When an emperor has lost his crown.
A clear lake reflects his image,
And a hill is seen in a distant sight.
He thinks of the country he managed,
Of how he lost it all in one fight.
A fallen emperor, exiled,
Bonaparte reflects on his days of glory,
On his empire that stretched for miles.
Now he simply stands, lonely.
And beneath constant watch from his foe,
The little Frenchman finally knows
That he is but a prisoner of Britannia
On the island of St. Helena.

PRESERVE

by Kaitlyn Truong

Oblivion nears as will subsides
Live your days out on a whim
And you'll find yourself falling in
Cherish close ones as if the sun won't rise
Exist with them as you would your kin
For life is fleeting and time is thin

JUDGMENT

By Hillary Nguyen

CHARACTERS

Zenith, sportscaster, god

Haya, sportscaster, god

Castor, mid-twenties male

Dante, deputy sheriff

Extras, police officers

FADE IN:

SETTING

INT. INTERROGATION ROOM - DAY

Camera focused on an interrogation room, zooms out to white room where there is a table with two gods, ZENITH and HAYA seated in professional attire. Behind them is a large screen of the interrogation room.

ZENITH

Thanks for joining us, folks. I'm Zenith, reporting live right above the interrogation room at the Berkshire County Station. And Haya is also here—as always—to comment on the upcoming events.

HAYA

Always great working with you, Zenith. It's now eight to four. The time for judgment.

ZENITH

That's right. Never a boring day here. Seems like we're working with yet another case of suspected homicide.

HAYA

The star of today's show is Castor. Will he end up flying in the clouds, or burning down underground? What do you think?

ZENITH

The odds are pointing down, down, down. He's a suspect for a murder case, where three bodies were found. The police claim to have found some significant evidence pointing to him, although they haven't yet revealed the details to the public.

HAYA

We're also working with what we can. The higher-ups still haven't disclosed whether Castor is actually guilty. His next actions will determine where his soul ends up, but if he can convince them to pardon him, his judgment will be delayed.

ZENITH

Well, if he's looking to go free then it'll be an uphill battle, especially if the evidence turns out to be good…

BACK TO: INTERROGATION ROOM

CASTOR is led by police officers into the room. He sits down, facing an already seated deputy sheriff DANTE.

ZENITH (V.O.)

Here he is, folks. Doesn't look too concerned about the accusations. He's having a staredown with Deputy Sheriff Dante.

HAYA (V.O.)

It looks like Castor's going on defense. Doesn't want his emotions to get the better of him. It's a deadpan expression that blocks out everything else. Common sight for some innocent folks in other cases we've seen.

ZENITH (V.O.)

Also a common sight for murderers who show no remorse—if you ask me, I think that's more likely. Now, for committing three murders without remorse, he won't just be burning in eternal flames.

HAYA (V.O.)

We'll get to that if it comes. It looks like Dante's making a move.

Dante slides an open laptop across the table.

ZENITH (V.O.)

Ooh, Dante's showing something… Well, it's probably just some post online.

HAYA (V.O.)

Wait, I see a flicker of anger in Dante's eyes. He's clenching his jaw. It's clearly not just a post.

ZENITH (V.O.)

We're zooming in on the laptop. Looks like a video of Castor arguing with one of the victims a week before the homicide.

HAYA (V.O.)

Castor's trying to convince Pollux to leave his gang and come home with him. Pollux refuses numerous times and it seems he's done with words. Pollux lands a right hook, and Castor staggers back. He keeps backing away while trying to calm Pollux down.

ZENITH (V.O.)

It's definitely more than just a sibling spat. Pollux just pulled out a knife… and Castor's still reluctant to fight back. He's still weak against family, eh? Boring.

HAYA (V.O.)

Pollux swings the knife but Castor dodges. Although he can't keep that up. Castor's now backed against a dead end. He's hesitating but wrenches the knife out of Pollux's hand and slashes him on the shoulder.

ZENITH (V.O.)

Anndd Castor runs away, knife still clenched in his hand. How anticlimactic. Was that really it?

HAYA (V.O.)

Not yet. Dante's pulling something out of a briefcase. It's the same knife from that fight and the knife found near the crime scene. Dante's smirking. He thinks that this'll pull some new info out of Castor.

ZENITH (V.O.)

Castor's keeping up his defenses and remaining silent. Definitely a hard wall to break through. It's back to the staredown again, unless Dante has another trick up his sleeve.

HAYA (V.O.)

It doesn't seem like it. In the meantime, let's give our viewers some background on Castor. Zenith, start us off.

CUT TO: WHITE ROOM

ZENITH

Sure thing. Castor had a spotty family life with one parent dead and the other dead-drunk. His twin ran away as a child. The man practically raised himself.

HAYA sets pictures of a younger Castor on the table.

HAYA

As a kid, he participated in illegal boxing rings. Not the worst offense, so he wouldn't be here if it were just that.

ZENITH

But things got a lot worse for him when he broke up with his ex, a prominent member of a local gang, the same one Pollux happened to join.

HAYA

Castor's been in a couple of fights because of that, but nothing on a large scale until recently.

ZENITH

He might not have done much else, but murder is still a pretty bad thing to have on your record.

HAYA

Well, the evidence is pointing to self-defense. The deaths are Pollux and other gangsters sent by Castor's ex. Allegedly, they blocked Castor in an alleyway. Not exactly touching for their second family reunion.

ZENITH

Self-defense will definitely lighten the sentence. Impressive that he took on three guys at once, though. I would've loved to give commentary on that.

HAYA

We work with what we have. We'll keep you posted, but before then, a word from our sponsors.

Switch to commercial (lie-detecting gadgets at your disposal…)

CUT TO: WHITE ROOM

ZENITH

We're back reporting live above the Berkshire County Station where things have been getting quite heated.

CUT TO: INTERROGATION ROOM

Dante stands up and slams a fist on the table. Castor clenches his fists and glares at Dante.

DANTE

Just confess and get a lesser charge. All of the evidence points towards you. We have witness testimonies from several people.

CASTOR

What witnesses? There was no one else there.

DANTE

Passing civilians saw you leave the crime scene. No one's on your side. You're wasting my time and yours.

CASTOR

At least we agree on something.

DANTE

You can't protest your innocence. Three people are dead because of you.

CASTOR

And you think I wanted to do—

DANTE

So you did do it. Took you long enough to admit the truth. Face it, your own brother is dead because of you.

Castor flinches.

CASTOR

I didn't want to! I never wanted to hurt him but… I was gonna… I never meant to ki—

Castor chokes up and looks down at the table.

DANTE

That doesn't change anything. You still did it and it's high time for justice.

Castor grits his teeth.

CASTOR

Shut up…

DANTE

There's nothing else to say, is there? Pollux is dead and it's your fault.

Castor stands up and punches Dante in the face.

ZENITH (V.O.)

Looks like things are blowing up now.

HAYA (V.O.)

Castor's lost control of his emotions. That defense crumbled in just a few minutes. Seems he still cared for his brother, despite everything.

ZENITH (V.O.)

Dante's on his feet now, trying to block Castor.

HAYA (V.O.)

Castor throws an uppercut at him. Dante takes the hit hard and steps back.

Dante grabs a walkie-talkie.

DANTE

Back-up. Interrogation room. Now.

ZENITH (V.O.)

Dante's just called for back-up. Can Castor fend for himself?

HAYA (V.O.)

Castor advances while Dante's distracted. A straight punch to his abdomen.

ZENITH (V.O.)

But Dante dodges and look, here comes the back-up.

Two police officers burst into the room.

HAYA (V.O.)

They're all cornering Castor. One slip-up and he'll be on the ropes.

ZENITH (V.O.)

It's a repeat of the past! What'll be his next move?

HAYA (V.O.)

A police officer makes a jab at Castor. Castor ducks and dodges.

ZENITH (V.O.)

Castor's pummeling through them. He's not backed up against the wall anymore.

HAYA (V.O.)

He's dodging hooks and jabs one after the other. Lovely footwork there. He'd make short work of the hellhounds underground. And looks like one officer is already knocked out cold. Got his head slammed against the wall after a hard shove from Castor.

ZENITH (V.O.)

A police officer is taking something out—oh! is that—oh, it's a Taser!

HAYA (V.O.)

That thing looks to be more than 50k volts. It'll definitely hurt if he lands a hit.

ZENITH (V.O.)

Castor's grabbing Dante and hurling him at the officer with the Taser. *Ooh*, wouldn't want to be in his shoes—Dante's gotta be hurting now. And look at Castor go! With a twist and a kick, both Dante and the Taser officer are down. Absolutely useless back-up on their part. And that third officer is still out cold.

HAYA (V.O.)

Castor's heading straight for victory. Seems all that time fighting has given him some seriously nice reflexes.

ZENITH (V.O.)

Can't forget about how terrible the police are, but it looks like all the commotion alerted everyone else.

More police officers burst into the interrogation room.

HAYA (V.O.)

Castor's been doing amazing against three officers, but it's impossible for him to fight off ten. He's on the ropes for sure.

Police officers tackle Castor. He's handcuffed and dragged away.

BACK TO: WHITE ROOM

ZENITH

Anndd that's a wrap, folks. Castor's in a cell now.

HAYA

As for his judgment…

ZENITH

After putting on such a great show, there's no way he's going to hell! It'd be such a waste.

HAYA

Castor would be a wonderful addition to the workforce.

ZENITH

So purgatory it is.

HAYA

Not the worst outcome today. Stay tuned for an exclusive interview with the ghosts of Castor's twin and the gangsters he murdered. Now then, another word from our sponsors.

FADE OUT

Painting that Calms the Storm

by Kayla Phatsavong

Anger creates chaos in my mind
Brush clashing with every stroke and line
Swirling thoughts like an ocean
As I live through the motions
Giving me peace that I can find

Carnage

by Bethanie Luu

Through smoke and ashes
Singing voices pierce
An open night's sky.
The world is my canvas,
And by crimson, I paint
To a chorus of shrieks
And exploding fireworks.
For in carnage, I bloom.

DEALING WITH THE DEVIL IN DISGUISE

by Kayla Phatsavong

I faced the devil on my own
Through manipulation and lies
The fear of feeling trapped
Had me scared for my life

I felt like a puppet on a string
There was no escape for me
Her burning desire to control
Conflicts ending in violence

She used me for my presence
But didn't care for me
I left home happier and free
But sometimes I pity her

She saw me as a reflection,
Not as a mother but as a friend
There was no love between us
Hard to tell if she really cares

DANCE FOR ONE

by Maria Tran

you thought I wouldn't be
able to dance alone.
so I did.
I danced till my feet hurt,
tangoed till I was out of breath,
spun till I dropped to the floor.
I did all of this to show you
that I don't need you
like you thought I did before.

EGGS

by Maria Tran

you cracked the egg so effortlessly.
it was as if you'd done it before.
you watched as the yolk dripped from its shell.
you knew it was delicate
just like my heart,
and yet you still broke it.
you watched tears run down my face,
only to break me again,
and again,
and again
until you had enough.
threw me out like i was rotten,
moved on to the next.
the newer, fresher egg.
and now i find you cracking eggs again,
one by one as their yolks spill out.

Born Again

by Hillary Nguyen

If I am born again, I want to disappear.
To have my atoms
disperse
and
detach
And settle
among the stardust
in the galaxy
For I know that I am but a speck of dust
That will never make an impact here.
I will never be remembered
But that's all right.
I will drift in the darkness of the nebula.
I will become a part of something,
More than I've ever been before.
But now I've found a different truth.
One that made me hesitate.
It kept me grounded
And now I know how helpless I am.
No matter what I do, in this lifetime
I will never be able to make up for it.
If I am born again, I want to live.

Stagnant

by Brian Ly

No gift will shine unless polished, it is said,
Yet there are the gifted who shine with ease.
Conversely, there are the unfortunate,
Ordinary, average, dull.

The dull can become exceptional, it is argued,
And I truly would love to agree.
Though I have tried to improve,
I have failed to see the fruits grow.

It takes time, just keep pushing, it is advised,
But that advice is no longer well received.
Smothered by encouragement, I'm suffocating.
Surrounded by a sea of talent, I'm drowning.

My motivation, gone.
My morale, destroyed.

I'm left drifting on a broken raft
Held together by a dying desire
Which blinds me from the harsh truth,
That my fruits are rotten,
That my talents lie stagnant.

OUTSHONE

by Jasmine Bui

The moon spills its bright white glow
Through the soft swirling clouds
And I stand here staring solemnly so,
In longing and lingering interest.
How is it still so that
The lights of the city shine even brighter,
Than that of the moon?
Sweeping, slowly, the buildings light up one by one
They glint, gleam, and glimmer,
But it has only just begun.
The stars with their own luminescence,
Try as they might to help the moon,
Cannot with all their essence
Even attempt to attune at why,
Just why, they are always outshone.

And as arbitrary as it seemed
There was no need to redeem
What they thought they had lost.
It wasn't the sky against the city,
It was the city against the lights,
The stars against the sand,
The moon against the night.

And there was some delight
In knowing that all of this showed
How those who aren't against it
Will be the ones that know—
Who is outshining whom.

THE WINDOW SEAT

by Bryce Le

THE CAFE BELL RINGS as I burst through the door, dripping water all over the welcome mat. The woman behind the counter glances up at me, an eyebrow raised, and I grin sheepishly as I look around the room. The only people in the building are me and the barista—which is to be expected, really, it's midnight and I'm amazed that this place is even open at all. Still, it's a very cozy place—everything is made of wood, there are plants all around the room, and lanterns hanging from the ceiling bathe the room in a warm glow. On the wall, a chalkboard menu hangs next to an old clock.

"Sorry about the rug," I say. "Rain hit me at a bad time. Mind if I stay here 'til it stops? I'll buy a drink." I was getting thirsty anyway.

The barista simply nods, pointing over to a booth by the window. In the daytime, it would probably have a lovely view of the streets, of the people walking by, but right now, there's nothing outside the window except darkness. The plush seats look inviting, though first I head to the counter and have a look at the menu on the wall. It's nearly illegible.

"Going to be entirely honest, I have no idea what that menu says," I tell the barista. She giggles silently. She hasn't said anything this entire time. "I'll just take whatever you recommend."

She nods and gestures again towards the window seat, before heading into the back, towards what I assume is the kitchen. I sink into the seat, and it is every bit as comfortable as it looked. Soft enough to fall asleep in, feels like sitting on a cloud.

Before long, the barista comes back out again, mug in hand. She leaves it on my table, and, without a word, heads back behind the counter.

"Thank you," I say. Again, she only nods. I look inside the wooden mug, and it's filled with tea. Tea. In a wooden mug.

Odd, but whatever.

I take a sip and freeze. A warmth spreads through my body, banishing the cold from me. I never was much of a tea drinker, but this is something fantastic. I'm… calm. Relaxed. The stress melts away, and I sit there in peace until my reverie is broken by a cough. A man stands next to my booth.

"Excuse me," he begins, "but would you mind if I took a seat here? All the other tables are filled."

"What are you talking about? This place is… empty…" I say, but as I look around I see that it very much isn't empty anymore. The cafe is packed with people, and a subdued chatter fills the air.

"…What?" I glance up at the clock. It hasn't moved, and I didn't hear any bell ring, so where did everyone come from? Before I can wonder more, the man clears his throat again. "Alright then, have a seat."

He slides into the booth, glancing out the window. "Thanks, friend. Terrible weather we're having, eh?"

"It's definitely something, that's for sure. In fact…" I scrutinize his clothing. "How are you not wet? It's pouring buckets out there." And yet, the man is dry as a bone.

He waves his hand. "Ah, that's not very important."

"Fine then. Keep your secrets."

We fall into a silence after that. I take some occasional sips from my mug of tea, while he continues to look out the window into the darkness outside. We stay like that for a while, until he opens his mouth again.

"So, do you think you're real?" he asks.

"Excuse me?"

"Do you think you're real?"

"What kind of question is that?"

He chuckles. "I'm just trying to make conversation, alright? Humor me a little."

"Fine." I look at him from over the lid of my mug. "I do think I'm real."

"And why is that?"

"I'm here, aren't I? I'm drinking this tea, I'm tasting it, and it's delicious. It all feels real enough to me. And besides," I take another sip. "There was that Greek philosopher who said something like 'I think, therefore I am,' wasn't there? I'm thinking right now, so I have to exist."

"His name was Descartes. French, not Greek."

"My point stands. And you?" I say, placing my mug down. "You think you're real?"

"I *know* I'm not."

Well, I certainly wasn't expecting that answer. What kind of person thinks they don't exist? I look over at the man again. At some point, he got himself a cup of coffee, without me noticing. "When'd you get that?" I ask him.

"That's not very important."

"You going to use that answer for everything?"

"Only the things that aren't important." He takes a swig from his cup, and I can *feel* the smugness radiating off of him, the kind of smugness that can only come from someone who knows that they know more than you, and knows that you know that.

I take another glance out the window. Still pitch black, still raining. At least the company in here is nice, even if he has some… interesting philosophies. "So why do you think you don't exist?" I say. It's nice to get some views from other folks once in a while, though I don't really think I'll be changing my mind on my realness anytime soon.

"I don't think. I *know*. And I know because…" He pauses for a while, staring at nothing in particular. "Well, it's hard to explain. Always is, I think."

"You say that like you've done this before. Do you just strike up philosophical conversations with strangers all the time?" What kind of person has the free time for that? Must be rich. Or unemployed. Either works, really.

"I'm not sure. I remember doing it, but—"

"If you remember doing it, then doesn't that mean you've done it?"

"Not really. It's like…" His eyes dart around the room, stopping on the door. "…when you forget to lock the door before leaving home. You obviously don't remember *not* locking the door, otherwise you'd have, well, locked it. Therefore, your mind would create a fake memory of you locking the door, because that's the only other thing you could have done, and so you drive away thinking the door is locked." He reclines on the chair, smirking.

"That is quite possibly the *worst* analogy I have ever heard." I stare at him, bewildered. "It doesn't even make any sense in this context. Having memories of a whole conversation is way different from memories of putting a key into a hole."

"Well it's more than what *you've* got." He grumbles.

"The hell is that supposed to mean?" I had memories. Had them right in my head, where they were supposed to be.

He leans forward, smirking. That smug aura is back in full force. "What did you do before you came into this cafe?"

"I was running from the rain, of course." That was only about half an hour ago.

"I see. And what were you doing before that?" That was an easy question. Before I got here, I was… I…

What was I doing, exactly? I had to be coming from *somewhere*. It's not like I just popped into existence in the rain, right?

"Don't know, huh?" The man stares at me intently. "Then tell me this: where are we?"

"That's an easy question. We're in a cafe."

"No name?"

"What, do you think I looked at the sign? It was dark and it was raining, I just ran in."

He frowns. "Fine, then. Where is this cafe located?"

I look outside again. It's so dark that I can't even see the street. All there is is the darkness and the rain on the window.

"We're in—" I begin, but I cut myself off when I realize that I don't know. What country are we even in? We're on Earth, surely, but I can't remember anything more specific than that. The man simply sits there, an inscrutable expression on his face. "I…" I shrug. "Well, I'm not sure, actually. Odd."

"Well then," he says, taking a sip of his coffee. "Final question. Do you know your name?"

It was a simple question. It was the kind of question you could ask a child, and they'd just look at you with a face that said "Of course I do, I'm not an idiot." I'm smarter than a child, at least I hope so. And yet, when I think of the question he asked…

I don't know.

I don't know my own name.

The man looks me dead in the eye. "You don't know, right?" He doesn't wait for me to confirm—he knows that I don't. "You don't know because you don't have one. It… well, I know you hate this phrase by now, but it wasn't important."

"I don't understand. It shouldn't matter if it's important or not." Everyone has a name, importance had nothing to do with it.

"I don't have one either, you know." His gaze is a bit softer now. "Nobody here does. In fact," he says, gazing around the room. "Have a look at them." He points towards the group sitting in the booth behind me, and my gaze follows. They seem blurry, like they're out-of-focus on a camera. They make noise, but I can't understand a word of it.

"Poor saps," the man continues. "Weren't even important enough to get an actual conversation written for 'em. You get what I was saying before now?"

I understand. But I don't want to. I refuse to. "How can we not be real? I'm here. I'm holding this cup. I'm feeling this cup in my hands, I'm hearing you talk, I can taste the tea in my mouth. How can none of it be real?"

He smiles weakly. "I suppose it all depends on your definition of 'real'. We're real words on a real page, but—" I glare at him. "But that's not really what you mean, is it?"

"So we're just…"

"A story. Written by an author who couldn't even care enough to give us names."

I stare into my tea. It doesn't taste nearly as nice anymore—it tastes like nothing, like I'm drinking a cup of water while someone next to me describes tea. I shove the mug away. "Is this how you felt when you found out?" I ask him.

"Wouldn't know. I've always been like this. In fact…" He leans closer to me, "got a suspicion that I didn't even exist until a couple dozen minutes ago. Earliest thing I've got clear memories of is seeing you at this booth."

"If that's how it works, then doesn't that mean that I didn't exist until I opened the doors to come in here?" If that's true, then I'm only about an hour old, technically. Not sure how to feel about that.

"I'm more worried about something else, to be entirely honest." For the first time, I can see a hint of apprehension slip into his visage. "We didn't exist until the story started, and that's—well, that's its own brand of unpleasantness, really—but all stories have to come to an end, don't they?"

A chill runs down my spine. "What happens to us then?"

"I imagine we go back to what we were before. Nothing." He furrows his brow. "Or we die and go to some afterlife. Or we end up trapped in this cafe for the rest of time. It could be anything, really. I'm as blind as you on this matter."

"All of those possibilities sound equally terrible, if you ask me." I stand up, surveying the room. The not-quite-people still sit at their tables, saying their not-quite-words, and the barista has disappeared into the back. "Think there's anything we can do to stop it?"

The man simply sits there, calmly sipping at his coffee. "Nothing that I can think of. You're free to try, but as for me," he chuckles, "I'll just keep savoring this drink."

"You're not going to help?"

"Why should I?" He answers. I look back at him, an eyebrow raised. I don't see any reason why he *wouldn't* want to help.

"Well, for one, we're both going to die if we don't stop it."

He just takes another sip of his coffee. "In any other situation, that would be enough. But tell me," he says as he sets down his drink. "What are you going to do?"

"For starters, I'm getting out of this cafe." I walk towards the front door. "You coming with me?" He doesn't move an inch. "Ugh… look, I'd really rather not be alone when I get out of here." I pull on the front door. It doesn't budge. I push against it, but it's stuck closed. It doesn't even move in the doorframe. Almost like it's just a wall in the shape of a door.

"If the door doesn't work, then how did I…" I glance around the room again. The door to the back of the cafe is closed. I run over to it, but it's jammed just like the front door. "Damn. Figures."

"Are you done yet?" the man asks. He's still drinking his coffee, seated at the booth next to the window. The very big, made of very breakable glass, window.

"One more," I grunt, lifting a stool up from in front of the counter. He simply looks on in amusement, while the not-people don't look at me at all. With a yell, I throw the stool at the window, and brace for the crash that is sure to follow.

The stool bounces off without leaving so much as a crack in the glass. Three exits to the cafe, and all are sealed. Nothing I can do.

I sigh as I sit down in front of the man again. He grins. "So how did it feel, wasting your energy for nothing?"

"At least I tried," I shoot back. "That's more than you can say."

"Why would I want to try? What will happen, will happen. It's inevitable. No point in trying to drag it out any longer." He takes another sip of coffee.

"That is a worryingly cynical perspective, isn't it?"

"If this were reality, I'd be inclined to agree. But it isn't, is it?" He gazes out into the nothingness outside. "This is just a story where the two of us are in a cafe and nothing happens. It can't be dragged on for long."

"But just sitting here and doing *nothing* like you," I grimace. "Doesn't sit right with me."

"And who said I was doing nothing?" He raises his cup. "I've been relaxing, savoring this fantastic coffee."

"That's all?" This was life-or-death, and here he was, drinking coffee.

He gestures around the room. "What else is there to do here? This coffee, this seat, they're the best I'm going to get." He pushes my mug of tea towards me. "When the time comes—and I'm sure it's coming soon, there's not much left to say—I'd like to say that I enjoyed myself the best I could. Wouldn't you?"

"I don't think I'm ready to just roll over and die. Not like you."

"Whether or not you're ready won't factor into it," he says. "The end comes regardless. The only thing you can decide is how you feel about it."

"There has to be *something* we can do—"

"But there isn't, is there? The finale to this story marches ever closer, even as we speak. Sit. Drink your hot leaf water." He hands me my mug.

"Why should I give up so easily?"

"What else can either of us do? Relax. Enjoy yourself. There's nothing more for us here."

I smile. A weak smile, but a smile nonetheless. "I suppose I don't have much of a choice, do I?"

I sit down and take a sip of my tea. It's delicious. Fragrant and calming.

Author Bios

Jasmine Bui

Both a reader and writer, Jasmine Bui grew up with a passion for the fictional world, taking interest in many genres, such as fantasy, romance, and adventure. She aspires to spread her ideas and creativity to the world through her art and writing, both of which are her main passions.

Vi Bui

An aspiring author and artist, Vi Bui has explored numerous creative outlets for years. Though most of her works remain in sketchbooks and word documents, this isn't her first time being published nor, hopefully, will it be her last.

Cecilia Dinh

Born and raised in Garden Grove, Cecilia Dinh developed a love for soccer, reading dystopian novels, and short story writing. "Ablaze" is her first published poem. In the future, she hopes to attend a good college and achieve her soccer dreams.

Khanhlam Doan

Originally born in Long Beach, Khanhlam resides in Fountain Valley along with her younger brother. She loves reading, biking, and collecting gemstones in her spare time. This year was her first foray into story-writing and she hopes to one day actually finish one.

Mia Gallardo

Born in California, Mia Gallardo grew up in Santa Ana and developed a passion for drawing and reading. She likes to have fun and joke around but is respectful to others. "Souls, Spring, and War" are her first published poems. In college, she plans to major in English.

Keanu Hua

With his inhibitions rarely corralled from a young age, Keanu Hua inspired by a morbid today works to create a bizarre, melding writing that ponders both the altruism and sacrifices of others and the ambitions of the successful.

An Huynh

An Huynh was born and raised in California with a love for literature, music, and drawing. Her works are often inspired by her thoughts and surroundings. When she's not coming up with ideas, An spends her time drawing and listening to music. She hopes to pursue a career in writing or pharmaceutical science.

Elaine Lam

Born in California, Elaine Lam is a hobbyist writer who works on personal novels on the daily and also frequently draws. It was in the summer of 2019 that she uncovered, through a song, a love for the blunt take on life. She wants you to be happy.

Bryce Le

Born in California, Bryce Le was raised in Westminster. They have an interest in writing and reading, and recently developed an interest in world building and fantasy. They'd like to be an engineer, but would take pretty much any job given to them.

Bethanie Luu

Bethanie Luu from California has a passion for figure skating, literature, and video games and an imagination as vast as the sea. Though she's hidden most of her works until recently, she hopes to share more of herself with the publication of her poems "Secrets" and "Carnage."

Brian Ly

Having spent just shy of half his life in California, Brian Ly is yet again attending a writing class; however, with 2020 being how it was, free time and boredom has led this lad into drawing more so than writing. Regardless, his contributions to this anthology include short poems and endless hours of editing.

Brandon Nguyen

Born in Garden Grove and raised there, Brandon Nguyen enjoys videogames and reading nearly anything. He writes stories to share his ideas and morals instead of entertainment. He hopes to live in Europe one day and to change someone's perspective through writing.

Christopher Nguyen

Born in California, Christopher, better known as Chris, grew up in Santa Ana where he developed a passion for working out and going camping. His first ever story, "Invasion," was praised by his middle school teachers. Chris aspires to move out of his parents' house and to travel the world with friends.

Hillary Nguyen

Hillary Nguyen grew up in Fountain Valley, California where she developed an interest in writing and drawing. She expresses her fantasy-centered imagination and random thoughts through her short stories and digital art. She hopes to further develop her art, writing, and coding skills and to also create games, comics, and visual novels.

Kayla Nguyen

Originally from California, Kayla Nguyen grew up in Westminster where she developed her passion for reading and writing. She hopes to improve her writing skills while making time for other creative pursuits like drawing. Her goal for this year is to finish a draft for a novella.

Michelle Nguyen

Michelle Nguyen has lived in the same house in Westminster, California her entire life. She grew up as an only child and found herself bored very often, so she took to many hobbies such as swimming, roller skating, and writing. "Dozing" and "Burnout" are her first published poems.

Stella Nguyen

Stella Nguyen grew up in California and loves beaches, swimming, singing, and reading. While she has written many stories in her head and on paper, her passion is poetry. Stella aspires to adopt an animal companion, be it mammal or reptile.

Vinh Park

Vinh Park was born in Vietnam, and moved to Orange County in the third grade. He enjoys gaming, writing short stories and watching movies in his free time. He really loves his friends and family, and would love nothing more than to see them be happy.

Kayla Phatsavong

Kayla Phatsavong has spent her life growing up in Garden Grove, California and becoming increasingly curious about the world and human behavior. Writing is something that eases her mind when she can't verbally express her emotions. As far as reading goes, poetry is her preference.

Vincent Quach

An Aztec of class 2022, (and former Celtic from St. Barbara School), Vincent Quach finds that writing gives him tranquility. Besides writing, he loves cooking. Friends with LQ Creative Writers before him, he is inspired by them to craft his own stories. He is an Aztec with a purpose of telling inspirational tales.

Khanh Tran

Born in Northern California, Khanh Tran grew up in the city of Oakland before moving south to Westminster. He admires history as well as the art of writing. "The Fallen King" is his first published work. In the future, Khanh hopes to become a U.S Army Officer.

Maria Tran

Originally born in Iowa, Maria Tran moved to California at the age of nine where she developed a thirst for creativity. She loves to express herself through singing, dancing, and writing. One day, Maria wishes to be able to live a successful and fulfilling life with little to no limitations.

Jacqueline Truong

Jacqueline Truong, an aspiring author and poet, has two other passions: drawing and studying Japanese. Having previously been published in La Quinta High School's "Spacing Out" anthology, she strives to continue to share her written works with the world.

Kaitlyn Truong

Kaitlyn Truong grew up in Fountain Valley, California where she became fond of writing. She loves reading stories, kayaking, and spending time with family. One day, she hopes to become a pediatrician.

Hailey Zuniga

Born in California, Hailey Zuniga grew up in Westminster where they discovered a love for cosplay, drawing, and writing. Although they have written since fourth grade, their first published poems are "The Ocean" and "Fire vs Water." One day Hailey hopes to become a marine biologist.

www.ingramcontent.com/pod-product-compliance
Lightning Source LLC
LaVergne TN
LVHW051007080826
845145LV00009B/2503

* 9 7 8 1 7 3 2 2 3 0 9 3 4 *